HALF MOON
RANCH

STARLIGHT

Also by Jenny Oldfield
published by Hodder Children's Books

Horses of Half-Moon Ranch 1: Wild Horses
Horses of Half-Moon Ranch 2: Rodeo Rocky
Horses of Half-Moon Ranch 3: Crazy Horse
Horses of Half-Moon Ranch 4: Johnny Mohawk
Horses of Half-Moon Ranch 5: Midnight Lady
Horses of Half-Moon Ranch 6: Third-Time Lucky
Horses of Half-Moon Ranch 7: Navaho Joe
Horses of Half-Moon Ranch 8: Hollywood Princess
Horses of Half-Moon Ranch 9: Danny Boy
Horses of Half-Moon Ranch 10: Little Vixen
Horses of Half-Moon Ranch 11: Gunsmoke
Horses of Half-Moon Ranch 12: Golden Dawn
Horses of Half-Moon Ranch Summer Special: Jethro Junior

Home Farm Twins 1–20
Home Farm Twins Christmas Special: Scruffy The Scamp
Home Farm Twins Summer Special:
Stanley The Troublemaker
Home Farm Twins Christmas Special: Smoky The Mystery
Home Farm Twins Christmas Special: Stalky The Mascot
Home Farm Twins Christmas Special: Samantha The Snob
Home Farm Friends: Short Story Collection

Animal Alert 1–10
Animal Alert Summer Special: Heatwave
Animal Alert Christmas Special: Lost and Found

One for Sorrow
Two for Joy
Three for a Girl
Four for a Boy
Five for Silver
Six for Gold
Seven for a Secret
Eight for a Wish
Nine for a Kiss

STARLIGHT

JENNY OLDFIELD

Illustrated by
Paul Hunt

A division of Hodder Headline Limited

With thanks to Bob, Karen and Katie Foster, and to the staff and guests at Lost Valley Ranch, Deckers, Colorado

First published in Great Britain in 2000
by Hodder Children's Books

10 9 8 7 6 5 4 3 2 1

A Catalogue record for this book is available from the British Library

ISBN 0 340 77965 9

Typeset by Avon Dataset Ltd, Bidford-on-Avon, Warks

Printed and bound in Great Britain by
The Guernsey Press Co. Ltd, Channel Isles

Hodder Children's Books
a Division of Hodder Headline Limited
338 Euston Road
London NW1 3BH

1

'Poor old Lucky! Does the cold weather make you feel miserable?' Kirstie Scott asked.

Her palomino quarter-horse trudged along Coyote Trail at a snail's pace. He was up to his hocks in powdery white snow; his breath emerged as clouds of steam in the crisp, clear air.

'Oh, please!' Kirstie's friend, Lisa Goodman, protested. She was riding ahead on peppy little Jitterbug, enjoying each jagged icicle and sweeping snowdrift on the way. 'We're having a great ride up here, so don't give me this "poor old Lucky" stuff!'

'Why not? He hates this sub-zero trek. Look, his

ears are laid back and he's hanging his head real low.' Kirstie was on the point of taking pity on her horse, turning him back along the narrow trail and heading for home.

But Lisa clicked Jitterbug into a trot, taking a left turn up a fresh trail that led away from Five Mile Creek. Her lively sorrel made deep prints in the unmarked snow. 'How do you know it's the weather that's doing that to him? It could be a hundred different things slowing him up back there.'

'No, it's the snow,' Kirstie insisted. She reined a reluctant Lucky up the slope after Jitterbug and Lisa. 'Every winter it's the same. Come the first serious snowfall, he gives me the clear message that this isn't his kind of weather. He slows right down, gets picky with his feed, hates it when I make ready to saddle him up and bring him out on the trail.'

'Huh!' Lisa was too busy enjoying the winter wonderland sights of the Meltwater Mountains to pay much attention. She snapped a thick icicle from a nearby tree, bringing a heavy shower of snow down from the laden branch.

Sulky Lucky shied to one side and plunged into a deep drift so that Kirstie had to work hard to stay in the saddle and steer him back on to the trail.

'You're a sunshine kind of a guy, aren't you?' she cajoled, as he picked his snow-caked hooves high out of the drift. 'You like to feel the heat baking the earth!'

'Yeah, right!' Lisa still wasn't convinced. 'You're talking as if horses have feelings like we humans do. "Lucky hates winter and loves the summer", blah-de-blah!'

'They do. He does.'

Lisa glanced over her shoulder, her round face shining, her dark red hair tucked up under the broad brim of a black stetson hat. 'Say that again! Horses have feelings?'

'Sure they do!' As Lucky struggled in Jitterbug's wake, Kirstie stuck to her guns. 'Don't you know that a horse is one of the most sensitive creatures on this planet? A good mount loves to please; that's why he works so hard for his rider. And he hates it if you treat him bad. Also, he gets lonely just like we do if you put him in a corral all by himself–'

'OK, OK!' Grinning broadly, Lisa cut her short. 'I should've known better than to set you going on your favourite subject! It's just that I forgot for a second back there about Kirstie Scott's well-known love affair with the entire equine species!'

'Cynic!' Kirstie grumbled back good-naturedly.

Anyhow, it was true that she liked the horses at Half-Moon Ranch better than most people who visited the place during the vacation seasons. She urged Lucky forward with a tap of her heels against his flanks, brushing more snow down from the overhanging branches and feeling it trickle down the back of her jacket collar. 'Don't you know that a horse reacts to every movement and sound in the landscape, and to the least little thing his rider asks him to do?'

'C'mon, Jitterbug, hum the theme tune to your favourite TV show for me!' Lisa joked, leaning forward to whisper in the sorrel's ear.

'Very funny.' Determined not to let her friend have the last word, Kirstie rode up alongside. 'I'm talking seriously here and you know it. Jitterbug will respond to the smallest shift of your weight, the tiniest pressure on the bit.'

Her grey eyes sparkled as the icy wind blew stray strands of fair hair across her cheek. 'In fact, Lisa Goodman, between here and the ranch house, I'd say that horse of yours will pick up every single heartbeat you make!'

The debate went on along the frozen forest track, past the landmark of Whiskey Rock and out on to a high ridge from where the girls could see the distant, dazzling sight of Eagle's Peak rising in snow-covered splendour to 14,000 feet.

It continued on the homeward trek through four-foot drifts, across frozen creeks, until the sloping roofs of the ranch came into view and even Lucky picked up his sluggish pace. The palomino pricked up his ears and raised his head, found fresh speed and balance on the iced-over tracks.

'See, he's happy now!' Kirstie insisted, to prove her point. 'Mind you, he won't let me forget taking him out in a hurry. He'll be real mean for the rest of the day: stepping on my toes, pushing me up against the sides of the row-stalls, ignoring me every chance he gets.'

For a moment, as they rode between the barn and the low bunkhouse, heading for the empty corral, Lisa grew serious. 'You want to know my theory? It's that horses don't feel and think the way you say they do. In fact, what's happening is that the rider kinda transfers his or her own emotions to the mount. If *you're* sad, the horse acts like he's moping. If *you're* upbeat, he acts happy. What's that called? There must be a name for it.'

'Dunno. Anyhow, it's not true. Every horse has

its own individual personality.' Kirstie reined Lucky to a halt.

She'd spotted Cornbread, the stray kitten the ranch had adopted in the fall, sneak out of the tack-room across the yard. He was a yellow-brown tabby who seemed to revel in risking life and limb by darting within striking distance of certain horses' hefty kicks.

'Take Jitterbug, for instance,' she said as she slipped from the saddle and shot Lisa a sweet, wide-eyed look. 'She has this thing about cats . . .'

'Whoa!' Lisa cried as Jitterbug spied Cornbread and reared up. She clung to the saddle horn as the sorrel pawed the air then came down hard while the little cat turned tail and scooted.

'See: she can't stand the sight of 'em.' Kirstie grinned as Lisa slowly brought her horse under control. 'Whereas, from what I know of her rider, well, *she* just loves the cute little kitten to pieces!'

'Here, kitty, kitty!' The girls had unsaddled their horses and put them in the row-stalls to feed when Lisa called Cornbread out of the way of a smart silver trailer that had just entered the yard.

Instead of seeking refuge in her arms, the scatty kitten swerved in front of the giant tyres.

'Ouch!' Kirstie cringed.

But Cornbread made it to the house porch, where he sat on the mat breathlessly counting his nine lives.

'Who's this?' Lisa wanted to know.

Kirstie shook her head. 'Search me. I don't recognise the truck or the driver. But it looks like Mom's taking delivery of a new horse for the ramuda.'

'Weird time of year to do that,' Lisa commented. Two weeks before Christmas, with no guests around, this gap between Thanksgiving and the New Year was the quietest period at Half-Moon Ranch.

'Hmm.' Intrigued, Kirstie went forward to meet Ben Marsh, the head wrangler, who had just emerged from the tack-room. 'What's the deal?' she asked him quietly.

'The deal is, we're taking Starlight off of Chuck North's hands.' Ben gave her minimum information. Then he left her to ponder and walked with his rangy stride to greet the driver who had just stepped out of his cab. 'Hey, Chuck. How was the Shelf-Road on your way in?'

'Icy,' Chuck North admitted. Like Ben, he didn't seem like a man to waste words. Instead, head down and face hidden beneath the brim of his stetson, he strode round to the back of the trailer to open the door.

'Starlight must be the name of the horse inside there!' Lisa whispered. 'What is this; some kind of mystery?'

Again Kirstie answered with a shrug. No doubt they would get the answers later, probably around the supper table. But for now, the important thing was to get the horse out of the trailer and into the corral. So she focussed on watching Chuck North step inside to untie the lead-rope.

'I wonder what kind of horse he is!' Lisa strained to see into the dark trailer.

'Quarter-horse, I guess.' Kirstie expected the usual addition to the ever-expanding string of dude horses that Sandy Scott kept at the ranch. The new arrival would probably be fourteen or fifteen hands, sturdily built and even-tempered – exactly the kind of horse that cowboys had ridden on the range for a hundred and fifty years.

'Starlight's a pretty fancy name,' Lisa pointed out. 'Maybe this is something different. Maybe a thoroughbred?'

'You wish!' Kirstie knew that no way could the Scotts afford to buy anything with breeding. The guest ranch was doing good business, but not that good.

From inside the trailer, they could hear the loud clatter of hooves on the metal floor and they could see the whole vehicle rock as Chuck North eased the equine passenger towards the door.

Then the horse appeared in the dark frame and Kirstie and Lisa gave loud gasps.

'Oh, wow!'

'Gee!'

'What *is* that?' Lisa sighed in awestruck admiration.

Starlight stepped down from the trailer into the snow-covered yard. A light sorrel with a white star and socks, he was made like no other horse Lisa had ever seen.

For a start, there was a bright coppery tinge to his coat. And his thick mane and tail were a mixture of reds, golds and browns that gleamed in the winter sun. Then there was his wonderful face. His large eyes were dark as coal, his nose was dished, his nostrils wide and flaring above a sweet, soft mouth. And his slim frame and delicate legs . . . the carriage of his head above his arched neck . . . the liquid movement and flexibility of his whole body as he danced his way on the end of the halter rope towards the girls.

'Meet Starlight!' Ben grinned at their overawed faces. 'He's a pure bred Polish Arab. American quarter-horses: eat your hearts out!'

How? What? When? Where?

Kirstie and Lisa bombarded Sandy Scott with questions at supper. They sat around the table with Kirstie's older brother, Matt, Ben and Hadley Crane, the old-timer who had lived and worked at Half-Moon Ranch since Kirstie's grandfather's time.

'Hold it!' Kirstie's mom held up her hands in protest. 'Let me tell you the whole story from start to finish just as soon as we've finished eating.'

'Is that a dream horse, or what!' Lisa murmured. 'I mean, did you see the way he moved, like he was walking on air!'

'Hmm.' Matt snorted then munched on.

Lisa ignored him. 'He's so pretty! You can bet every single guest who visits the ranch next spring will take one look at him and want to ride him.'

A sniff from Matt, followed by more determined scraping of forks against plates.

'How come Chuck North wanted to part with a horse like that?' Kirstie asked, the moment her mom's cutlery hit the plate for the final time. She recalled the glow of his coat as they'd led him into the row-stalls for feed after his journey, his dainty, dancing gait as he covered the ground.

'He didn't exactly *want* to part with him,' Sandy explained. 'But there are a couple of reasons why they had to say goodbye. The first is, the Norths are in financial trouble over at Mile High Ranch, just outside Denver. They kept over a thousand head of cattle, but they still couldn't compete on prices with the really big guys. So Chuck is having to sell up and move on.'

'Not good!' Kirstie admitted. Maybe this was one of the reasons why Chuck North hadn't lingered in the yard once he'd unloaded Starlight, and why he'd refused coffee and simply turned the trailer around and headed back out along the Shelf-Road towards Route 3. Money problems didn't exactly make a man talkative.

'What's the second reason you offered Starlight a home?' Lisa asked.

'You think that's bad, but wait, it gets worse,' Sandy continued. 'Chuck and Marie bought him for their son, Jay – who must be around sixteen years old now, I reckon. I knew of the family when we lived in Denver way back. They bought Starlight for

Jay's eighth birthday, so the boy and the horse kinda grew up together.'

'Like me and Lucky,' Kirstie reminded them. Ever since the Scotts had moved out of the city to the ranch, six years earlier, the palomino and she had been inseparable.

'Right. There's a bond between them. Only, last summer Jay fell ill. They did lots of tests and finally discovered that he has some kind of leukaemia.'

'Gee, that sucks!' Lisa frowned then fell silent.

'Can they make him better?' Kirstie wanted to know.

'The doctors put his chances at fifty-fifty or so,' Sandy admitted. 'Better if they can find a bone marrow match, but that's not happening right now. Meanwhile, Jay is hospitalised for periods of chemotherapy and his parents have decided that it's just not practical to keep Starlight on at the ranch. That's why I offered to take him when I heard what their set-up was.'

'That's your problem, Mom, you're too sentimental in that way,' Matt put in quietly. 'You hear a sad story and you step right in, without taking into account what it costs us to keep an extra horse.'

Kirstie frowned and shot her brother a narrow look. Trust Matt to pour cold water on the situation.

'Yeah, well, it didn't cost us anything to acquire Starlight,' Sandy reminded him. 'The Norths let him go for nothing, knowing that we'd take care of him real good until the time maybe comes when they can take him back.'

Matt tutted. 'That's not the point. You only have to take one look at the horse to know he's not a natural trail horse. You put a dude rider on him and he'll buck him off before they leave the corral.'

'How do you know that?' Lisa quizzed, instinctively lining up with Kirstie and Sandy against hard-headed Matt.

'He's an Arabian, ain't he? And Arabians are wired wrong for guest riders. They're too highly strung; they spook at their own shadows. Besides they're not sure-footed enough on these mountains. It won't be a week before that horse breaks a leg, believe me.'

'But if he has a good rider who knows how to handle him, he'll be fine,' Kirstie pointed out. 'Ben just has to select carefully, that's all. Or maybe Starlight would make a permanent staff horse for you, Mom, or for Ben. Then you could be sure he had an expert rider on his back.'

Ben nodded thoughtfully, slower to give his

opinion, and turning instead to the old hand, Hadley.

'A horse like that, it don't winter well at this altitude,' the old man commented. 'Difficult to keep his weight up and all.'

'Hmm.' Ben nodded again. 'Sounds like I gotta get him on the Breakfast Club list already.'

Kirstie knew that horses in the Breakfast Club were brought in daily during the winter from Red Fox Meadow for extra feed with heavy grain content, instead of the normal alfalfa hay which was tractored out to the meadow and loaded into the open feed-stalls. But this was OK, Starlight wouldn't be the only horse in the herd who needed special attention. She tried to tell herself that, despite Matt and Hadley's reservations, Starlight had come to the right place.

But there was a niggling doubt nevertheless.

For starters, she had to admit this really wasn't like her mom, whose head for business had developed over the years to the point where she wouldn't take on a horse that might not pull its weight in the dude string.

And, as she walked out with Sandy to the meadow later that evening after Lisa had gone home to San Luis, Kirstie could appreciate Hadley's point that

Starlight might not survive the tough life at Half-Moon Ranch.

After all, the little sorrel was a lightweight, standing apart from the other horses in the ramuda, probably no more than 14 hands high, and delicate. More like a ballet dancer than a hundred metres sprinter, if you thought in human terms. Graceful, quick-moving, never still.

Mother and daughter stood at the fence of the meadow, under the moon and stars, eyes glued to the newcomer, thinking their own thoughts.

Starlight saw them and raised his head. He was dark against the white snowy background, almost a silhouette. Except they could pick out the paler mane and tail, the gleam of his coal-black eyes.

'What d'you think?' Sandy murmured without taking her gaze away from the Arabian.

He turned towards them, trotted a couple of steps, then dropped his head as if in disappointment. He veered away, to lope the length of the field and back. Then he stood looking up at the star-studded sky, ears pricked and listening.

'He's beautiful!' Kirstie whispered back.

'But will he fit in?'

Kirstie clenched her jaw tight. *Beautiful but yearning for home,* she thought, though she didn't say it. If she was honest, bringing Starlight to Half-Moon Ranch was like putting a sleek sports coupé alongside a row of Dodge pick-up trucks in a car sales lot.

'It's OK, you don't have to spell it out,' Sandy sighed, leaning on the fence, hands clasped.

'So, what's the real deal here?' Kirstie ventured. She sensed a heap of trouble in the air, and pain and sadness.

Sandy's voice broke a little as she replied. 'I just feel so sorry for the Norths,' she admitted. 'Imagine what it must be like to have your only son diagnosed with a potentially fatal disease.'

'Awful,' Kirstie agreed. *Unimaginable in fact.*

Her mom sighed and let her in to her innermost thoughts. 'The way I figure it is, we can keep the horse here for Chuck and Marie while Jay undergoes treatment. Then, wherever they end up, the best thing we can do is to return Starlight to the family just as soon as the poor kid gets back on his feet.'

2

'Good job!' Ben praised Kirstie for finally cornering Johnny Mohawk in Red Fox Meadow and buckling a headcollar on to him.

The high-spirited, almost black horse had given her a run for her money, allowing her to approach, only to swerve and duck out of reach at the last possible moment. But now he stood quiet, nuzzling at her shoulder and shoving her gently with the side of his head.

'Anyone would think I was gonna make you do some work instead of taking you in for extra feed!' Kirstie laughed, crooking her arm around Johnny's neck. 'Breakfast Club. That's what this is about, OK!'

Taking a firm hold of his lead-rope, she followed Ben and Navaho Joe across the trampled meadow towards the ranch buildings. These two were the last of the underweight horses needing the additional food, and they took them to join Lucky, Snowflake, Starlight and little Gulliver in the row-stalls.

The line of horses shifted restlessly in the narrow stalls. Each was tethered on a short rope, staring hopefully at the as-yet empty wooden mangers. Meanwhile, they jostled their flanks against the iron partitions, flicked their tails and stamped their feet.

'Breakfast coming up!' Ben announced. Having tied up Nav, the brown-and-white appaloosa, next to Starlight, he strode off into the barn to emerge soon after with a barrow load of small grain pellets and a large scoop. 'Over to you,' he told Kirstie, leaving her to do the honours.

The hungry horses snickered, then pushed and shoved some more. Kirstie dipped the scoop into the pellets and quickly poured them into Lucky's manger. The picky palomino curled back his upper lip and nibbled uninterestedly at the special rations.

'What did you expect; fresh alfalfa?' Kirstie chided. 'Well sorry, buddy, no-can-do!'

She went down the row, glad to see Gulliver, Taco's palomino colt, duck his head and gobble his food. The same with Snowflake and Johnny; the two of them crunched happily. But further along, she noticed Navaho Joe give Starlight a hefty kick between the iron bars of his stall. The unwary new arrival took the full force of the hind hoof on his nearest hock.

'Hey!' Kirstie paused in her work and went to take a look at the result: an inch-long, curved tear on Starlight's leg, just below the knee joint. Though it was a superficial wound, it would need antibiotic cream and a careful eye over the next couple of days.

'Great!' Kirstie grumbled at the belligerent appie. 'There's no need to get at Starlight just because he's new here. You were in the same situation once, remember!'

Navaho Joe tossed his head and pulled at his tether. *Feed me, feed me!*

So Kirstie tipped a scoop of pellets into his manger, then moved on to Starlight, who stood trembling slightly after the sudden attack. 'Sorry about that,' she murmured. 'Nav has no manners. He spent a few months running wild in the mountains, and he's still kinda wired up in survival mode. I guess he didn't know you and he was scared you were gonna steal his food!'

Sighing heavily, Starlight dropped his head towards the newly arrived pellets. He sniffed, then turned listlessly away.

'C'mon, you gotta eat!' she encouraged. 'With the temperature set sub-zero from now right until March, you're gonna need plenty of layers of fat to see you through.'

But the handsome Arab horse ignored the invitation. He simply hung his head, letting his multi-coloured mane droop over his dark eyes, breathing clouds of steam through his delicately flared nostrils.

'Hmm.' Kirstie took a step back. She considered Starlight thoughtfully. 'Not good,' she murmured.

Then she went off to the tack-room for antibiotic cream for the cut. *Maybe Starlight will settle after a couple of days*, she told herself. But as she returned with the cream and saw him from a distance, head hanging, shivering and miserable, she thought, *There again, maybe not*.

'Cut it out, Cornbread!' Matt snatched his white stetson from the floor of the tack-room where the young cat was playing. The kitten had knocked the hat from a ledge and dived underneath the crown to hide, until Matt had realised what was going on and shooed him off.

A few feet away, Kirstie grinned as she lifted her saddle down from its peg. 'Poor Matty; did the kitten spoil your nice new hat, then?'

'Yeah, and you can cut it out too.' Matt was in no mood for kidding. It was ten days to Christmas and he had a heap of college work to get through before he could relax into the vacation. This on top of mending fences, ordering feed, and bringing the accounts up to date for the ranch. So he brushed the dust from his hat, jammed it on to his head and stamped over to the ranch-house to begin an essay on the importance of de-worming products in the prevention of equine colic.

Staggering a little under the weight of the saddle, Kirstie stepped out into the corral. She slung the tack over a nearby rail, then went to seek out Lucky from the row-stalls. Her plan was to take him on a ride out along Five Mile Creek this Saturday morning, before driving into town with her mom.

But as she approached the Breakfast Club horses, a different idea entered her head. *Why ride Lucky, who was so reluctant to come out and enjoy the snow with her? Why not choose Starlight instead?*

After all, it would give her alone-time with the new horse, who, after three days at Half-Moon Ranch, was still feeding badly and looking lonely. Maybe she could set up some special connection with him, make him feel wanted and cared for in his new home.

But first, she had to check a couple of things. For a start, there was that cut to his leg, inflicted by Navaho Joe. Entering the furthest stall, Kirstie bent to inspect the wound. 'Good,' she muttered, noting that the flesh had healed over nicely.

So she went to find Ben, busy loading hay bales on to the trailer to take to the horses in the meadow.

'Hey,' she said casually. 'How about I take Starlight out on the trail this morning?'

The head wrangler paused mid-lift. 'What about Lucky? Won't he be madder'n a gut-shot possum to see you riding out on another horse?'

Kirstie grinned and shook her head, reminding Ben how the palomino hated the cold. 'I reckon I can rest Lucky over Christmas and concentrate on the Arabian. It'll do them both a whole heap of good.'

Ben tossed the bale on to the trailer. 'Hmm.'

'So, whadd'ya think?'

'I think, go ahead,' the wrangler agreed, terse as

ever. Then he jumped on to the tractor and drove away.

So it was Starlight who Kirstie led out of the row-stalls, appreciating his springy, Arabian-style walk, the lift of his tail, the arch of his neck. He moved smooth as silk and daintily, ears pricked expectantly, and when she tethered him to the rail to sling the saddle over his shiny, coppery back, he didn't flinch.

'Good boy!' she murmured, tightening the cinch. Then she fetched a bridle and carefully introduced the bit to his soft-looking mouth. 'Easy!' she whispered, hooking her thumb into the corner of his mouth so that he let his jaw drop open and she was able to insert the metal bar. Soon he was ready to mount.

'Lookin' good!' A whistle from Charlie Miller who was passing by with a giant scooping shovel drew a grin from Kirstie.

'Me or the horse?' she called.

'Both!' The young wrangler disappeared behind the barn to carry on with his chores.

'Be back by midday!' Sandy poked her head out of the house and yelled after Kirstie. She did a double-take when she saw her on Starlight.

'It's OK, I checked with Ben!' Kirstie insisted, feeling the bounce in the Arab's stride as he took the slope out of the corral. This was going to be a fun ride, she decided.

'Where do you plan to ride?' Her mom's voice trailed after her.

'To Angel Rock!' Kirstie yelled; another spur-of-the-moment decision.

Angel Rock – a special place for the staff at Half-Moon Ranch, unknown to guests and outsiders. Special because it was so beautiful and secluded, so off the beaten track. And just the sort of spot she thought Starlight would appreciate.

The snow sparkled in the sun like a million diamonds.

No one had trodden here in weeks, so the soft, white blanket was unmarked, except for the light tracks of a deer which criss-crossed the clearing.

All around, the tall ponderosa pines were laden with powdery snow which the breeze lifted in light clouds and blew against Kirstie and Starlight's faces.

She felt the icy powder melt against her warm cheeks, breathed in the pure smell of it, gazed up at the rock formation beyond the trees.

They stood in a tight semi-circle some thirty feet tall, making a sheer wall that hung now with long, clear icicles. To one side, a frozen waterfall hung in suspended animation – fingers of water six feet long, draped over a narrow rocky ledge and pointing to an iced-over pool below.

Beneath the ice, locked into winter, were patches of green fern and broad-leaved marsh plants, shiny pink boulders, smooth white pebbles.

And overlooking the whole silent scene was the rock in the shape of a Christmas angel which gave the place its name.

Some people saw it and others didn't. Matt, for instance, could never work out the shape of an angel in the conical structure.

'It's sideways on!' Kirstie would insist. 'You can see its wings sprouting out at the back, and its head, and its arms folded as if it's praying!'

'Yeah, yeah!' He would shrug and turn away. 'Like, my name's Santa Claus!'

You either got it or you didn't.

Kirstie saw an angel clear as day. It was set against the bright blue sky, head bowed, wings unfurled, looking down on this secret, frozen place.

And Starlight too seemed affected by the majesty of his surroundings. He stood quiet, head up but relaxed. There wasn't a twitch or a fidget throughout his entire body. And he was looking up

at the rock, paying attention, maybe even waiting for something to occur.

'Beautiful, huh?' Kirstie whispered. For the first time she sensed an ease and calmness in the nervy little gelding.

Starlight didn't shift. He stood gazing up at the angel, as if listening to a faraway voice.

'The poor guy's homesick; that's his major problem!' Kirstie told Lisa.

She'd driven into town with Sandy that afternoon and been dropped off at the End-of-Trail Diner, where Lisa lived with her mother, Bonnie Goodman.

And from the moment she'd arrived, she'd talked of nothing but Starlight.

Lisa went about the diner, placing ketchup bottles on tables. 'Anthropomorphism!' she said loud and clear.

The long, clumsy word stopped Kirstie in her tracks. 'Come again?'

'Anthropomorphism. It's what you're doing: giving an animal the characteristics of a person. Like we were talking about the other day; that animals have feelings and so on. I knew there must be a name for it, so I looked it up.'

'Like, I really needed to know that mouthful!'

'It's a well-known thing. Loads of people do it.'

'OK, so it must be true. Animals must have feelings, like I said.'

'Just because loads of guys believe it doesn't mean it's true.' Lisa rapped the final sauce bottle on to the checkered tablecloth. She was dressed in jeans and a white shirt, ready to give her mom a helping hand when the diner grew busy later in the afternoon.

'Believe me, Starlight is homesick for Mile High Ranch!' Kirstie overrode her friend's doubts. But she wasn't certain that she should confide in her about the sad moments at Angel Rock, when it had seemed to Kirstie that poor Starlight's heart might actually be breaking.

The little sorrel had gazed at the angel for minutes on end, heaving great sighs and standing unnaturally motionless.

'Well, tough.' Unhooking a blue-and-white striped apron from behind the counter, Lisa tied it around her waist. 'Starlight had better get over it because from what I hear, the Norths have already moved out.'

'That's right!' Bonnie Goodman swept in on the girls' conversation as she pushed in through the diner door with a crate full of fresh milk cartons. She brought with her the freezing air of a cold December afternoon. 'As a matter of fact, Chuck and Marie North are in San Luis today, checking out places to rent.'

Lisa raised her eyebrows knowingly at Kirstie. 'Did you see them?' she asked her mom.

Both mother and daughter were heavily into town gossip, Kirstie knew. So she expected to be brought quickly up to speed on the Norths' situation.

'No,' Bonnie replied. 'But I just bumped into Sharon Werther from the realtor's office. She told me that Chuck North had been in early today, looking for properties. And she says he's a worried man.'

'Did she tell you they already had to give up the ranch?' Lisa picked up news like a sponge soaks up water.

Bonnie nodded. She talked as she loaded milk into the freezer. 'They want to move away from the city, out this way. Chuck thinks he might find work managing a ranch. It's a big step down from owning his own spread, but beggars can't be choosers, as they say.'

'And it's all happening just before Christmas; isn't that terrible?' Lisa sighed. She lowered her voice as customers entered the diner.

'Maybe Chuck will land a job with a house attached.' Bonnie took an order for three portions of waffles with crisp bacon and eggs over-easy, then went on in an undertone. 'I did hear from Sharon that Donna Rose at the Circle R was on the lookout for a new head wrangler.'

'Did somebody tell Chuck North that?' Lisa wanted to know.

Bonnie shrugged. 'Yeah, Sharon. But it seems he's maybe not too keen on taking his orders from a woman.'

As the diner slowly filled with people, the talk about the Norths' problems died away and Kirstie willingly helped out at the tables.

It was when she was clearing plates from one near the steamed-up window that she caught sight of what she took to be a familiar figure. She knew the man but couldn't place him, and certainly didn't recognise the woman and kid who walked along the sidewalk with him.

The guy went head down, face hidden underneath his hat, giving none of the usual greetings to local people.

The woman, small and heavily wrapped up in a black padded jacket, looked hesitant and unhappy.

And the boy, going along a step or two behind his parents, was thin, pale and silent.

The Norths! Kirstie put down the tray with a small rattle. Of course, the guy hiding behind the hat was Chuck North, as uncommunicative as when he'd dropped off Starlight at Half-Moon Ranch. He turned now to cross the street and she saw a broad-faced man with tight, narrow lips and frown lines etched in between his nose and the corners of his mouth. Marie North turned with him, perhaps a little older than her husband and quite plain, with her greying hair cut short around a thin, lined face.

The couple and their son were obviously doing their best to ignore the curious but not ill-meaning stares of the San Luis locals. Of course, everyone in the small town had heard the Norths' bad-luck story and they couldn't help concentrating their gaze on the sick son.

There but for the grace of God . . . Mothers and fathers counted their blessings, felt strong pangs of pity for the strangers in town with the son who had a death sentence hanging over him.

And the Norths kept on heading across the street, right for the door of the diner.

Kirstie gathered herself to pick up the loaded tray. She hurried to the counter, giving Lisa a significant look and nodding towards the opening door.

The bell rang. An icy blast of wind accompanied the latest customers.

People in the dinner couldn't help it; they weren't especially callous or interfering, but neither could they tear their gaze away from Chuck, Marie and Jay North. So they stared over their waffles and bacon, their coffees and Cokes.

'Hey there.' Bonnie greeted the Norths with a nervous smile. 'What can I get for you folks this freezing cold afternoon?'

3

The uneasy atmosphere in the End-of-Trail Diner held during the time that Chuck North placed his order.

While the bacon sizzled on the griddle and Bonnie flipped over half a dozen eggs, the three strangers took seats at the window table which Kirstie had just cleared.

'I'd like a cup of hot chocolate while we're waiting,' Marie said quietly, her face flushed, a knot of concentration between her fair eyebrows.

Close to, Kirstie saw that she was maybe not as old as she'd first thought; perhaps just under forty with prematurely grey hair. Taking a swift glance at Jay North, she found that he was a younger version of his mother – the same long, thin face and light brown eyes, only his hair was sandy coloured and his skin unmarked. Yet it had a peculiar, uniform paleness – almost waxy – and his eyes were hollow in their sockets.

'Black coffee for me,' Chuck snapped, interrupting Kirstie's close scrutiny of his son.

She jerked into action, glad to note her mom stepping through the door into the diner. Sandy paused to kick snow from her boots on to the sidewalk, then breezed across.

'Anything to drink?' Kirstie asked Jay before she left the table.

The kid shook his head without looking up.

'Hey, Chuck!' Sandy approached with a broad smile, for all the world acting as if the Norths were the people she most wanted to see in the whole world. She gave no sign of being uncomfortable as she sat down at their table and called Kirstie back to add an extra coffee to the order. 'Thanks, honey. This is my girl, Kirstie, in case you three hadn't recognised her from way back,' she rattled on, drawing Jay directly into the conversation. ''Course Kirstie was practically a babe in arms at the time, so no way would she remember you.'

'Hey,' he muttered, colouring up and still refusing to meet her gaze.

Sandy turned to Marie and Chuck. 'Is it true, you hope to find a place to stay around here?'

'We're thinking maybe we might,' Marie conceded. 'Everything's still up in the air, though.'

'Oh but it would be great if we got to be neighbours!' Sandy insisted. 'Remember the old days, when we lived in Denver; how I'd bring Matt and Kirstie out to Mile High when they were small kids? It looks like things could be about to turn around, so you can come visit us at Half-Moon.'

Her genuinely enthusiastic chatter helped the whole place to relax and get back to their burgers and fries.

'Your mom's one in a million,' Bonnie murmured quietly to Kirstie. 'See how she's making them feel like they already belong!'

Kirstie nodded. 'What's the latest on Jay?' she whispered, unable to refrain. The kid looked so quiet and pale still, even though both his parents had warmed up under Sandy's advances.

'They're still looking for a bone marrow donor,' Bonnie told her. 'The doctors reckon that if they don't find a match by early in the New Year, then the kid's chances dip down well below evens.'

Feeling her heart tighten at the grim news, Kirstie watched Jay get up from the table and walk awkwardly to the slot machine by the door. He inserted a coin and began to play, to the whizz and clatter of the sound effects on-screen.

In a pale imitation of her mum's warm friendliness, Kirstie decided to approach Jay.

'Hey,' she said casually, taking used plates from the nearest table.

He didn't look up or offer any reply.

'I guess you must be missing your little Arabian sorrel,' Kirstie blundered on, trying to make contact.

She saw Jay flinch and miss the cue on-screen.

'I mean, who wouldn't? Starlight is definitely in the running for the best looking horse of all time contest!'

Garbage! How come she opened her mouth and this stupid stuff came gushing out?

The kid closed his eyes and leaned for a moment on the glass lid of the played-out machine.

'Don't get me wrong; he isn't just a pretty face. I took him up to Angel Rock this morning and he went like a dream . . . !'

'Erm, Kirstie!' Lisa passed by and saw the

disastrous effect she was having. 'Back off, huh?'

Taking a deep breath, she nodded then added, 'Come over to the ranch and see Starlight any time you want.'

Jay turned to face her for the first time. There was anger in his hazel eyes, a tiny flush of colour in his waxy face. 'Would that visit be before or after the major, life-saving surgery I may or may not get to have?' he asked.

'Not your fault,' Sandy insisted as she and Kirstie worked together in the barn last thing that night.

In their absence, Hadley had checked with the weather station and discovered that a fresh fall of heavy snow was due overnight and he'd taken it upon himself to bring in the least sturdy horses from the meadow. These included Gulliver, Johnny and of course Starlight.

'Not that I want you thinking that I'm going soft on these critturs,' he insisted. 'Only, Gulliver here took a kick to his ribs from that gangster, Nav. Johnny's way under his summer weight and has no protection against a temperature of fifteen degrees below. And Starlight; well, you know . . .'

Kirstie glanced at the Polish Arab; thin and miserable as ever. She went up to him to rub his neck and re-establish the bond she hoped they'd formed on the ride to Angel Rock. But she found that Starlight simply turned his handsome head and wandered listlessly to the far corner of his straw-strewn stall.

'You want to know the real problem with him?' Hadley took up the subject with Kirstie after Sandy had checked the row of box-stalls.

'No,' she sighed, spotting one of Hadley's rare lectures on the near horizon. Normally the old man kept his thoughts to himself, except when the subject was horses and a situation was on the point of becoming urgent.

'It's the old story about pecking orders,' he insisted, speaking in a long, slow drawl. 'Y'know; herd mentality and fixing who's the boss.'

'What does that have to do with Starlight?' In spite of her reluctance to be lectured, Kirstie had to ask.

'A horse is a herd animal, OK? They stick together and when danger approaches, they flee to safety.'

'Yeah. So?' By this time Kirstie had slipped in to Starlight's wooden stall to fuss around with his straw bedding.

'So there's one horse in control of every herd. Almost always a female; the dominant mare.'

'Like Hollywood Princess in our ramuda?'

Ever since the American Albino's arrival from Echo Basin in Wyoming, Hollywood had established herself as the major power in the ramuda.

'Hollywood; right. Now she sees a new arrival like Starlight here. He's not like the rest of them – plain ordinary quarter-horses. No, he's special. But he's not real big and he's sure not tough. So Hollywood can pick him out for a little rough treatment. Nips, bites, kicks and so on. She can even encourage bully boys like Navaho Joe to pick on him too.'

'Is that why you brought him in from the meadow?' Kirstie asked, increasingly worried. She ran a hand along Starlight's back to check for bites and bruises.

'Let's just say I'm uneasy about the politics out there,' Hadley conceded. 'I found Starlight here cornered up against the fence, with Nav and Chigger in a stand-off, two against one. I don't like to think what I might've found if I'd left it five minutes longer.'

'So what're you saying?'

'I'm saying it don't look good for the little guy. On top of the problem he has with his size and the pretty-boy looks, there's the fact that he's pining for home.'

Kirstie's deep intake of breath showed that she agreed. 'It's like he's here at Half-Moon Ranch, but not here. Present in body, but not in mind. I guess he's fretting over Jay.'

'Likewise, the kid must get gut-ache real bad whenever he thinks about the horse.' After a lifetime working with horses, getting bucked off unbroken colts, mastering them then riding the range together for weeks at a time, no one understood better than Hadley the bond between horse and rider.

'You'd think,' Kirstie agreed. Then she described Jay's reaction to her blundering attempts to fill him in on Starlight's situation. 'He gave me this blank stare and knocked me all the way back into Main Street. No questions, no sign of interest. It was like he just didn't care.'

'Hmm.' Hadley grunted, then turned out the light shining into Starlight's stall. 'The kid cares,' he insisted. 'Believe me, he's missing that little guy worse than you'll ever know!'

The snow didn't come that night as forecast. Kirstie woke on the Sunday to look out of her bedroom window and see heavy, swollen clouds settled over Eagle's Peak but no fresh fall on the ground.

'They say it's gonna hold off for twenty-four hours,' Matt told her over breakfast. 'Time for a drive in to town to watch a movie if you'd like.'

Kirstie gave him a sideways glance, wondering how come he'd suddenly developed a generous streak. 'Since when did you undergo a personality transplant?'

Her brother flicked his hand across the top of her head, mussing up her hair. 'I didn't. I plan to ride in to San Luis this afternoon to meet up with Lauren anyways.'

The New Girlfriend. Lovely Lauren. Kirstie knew Matt would snatch every chance to spend time with her. 'That figures!' she laughed, accepting the lift in any case.

And so, after a morning crammed with chores in the tack-room and stables, they set off together along the narrow Shelf-Road. Matt's rusty old car rattled over the frozen ridges and skidded perilously close to the sheer edge, recovering just in time to steer away from a rocky drop into a white gulley stiff with icicles, its creek frozen solid under a six-inch sheet of ice.

Kirstie braced both arms against the dashboard and held her breath. 'You need skid-chains on these tyres,' she complained, sounding worryingly like their mom.

'Yeah, yeah.' Matt drove on unconcerned, playing loud country music on the radio, tapping the steering-wheel as they bumped and rattled on.

'Remind me never to take a ride with Matt ever again, would you?' Kirstie stepped out of the car on to the sidewalk outside the End-of-Trail Diner, her legs like jello. She practically fell into Lisa's waiting arms.

On Matt's radio a cowboy wailed a lyric about losing the love of a good woman and ending up in the jailhouse.

'Look what you did to my friend!' Lisa grinned at him. 'How's she ever gonna get it together to come and watch a horror movie with me?'

'No, please!' Kirstie made a big thing of wobbling and shaking along the sidewalk. 'Not a *horror* movie!'

With a shrug and a wave, and promising to pick Kirstie up again at six-thirty, Matt cruised off down the street to his meeting with Lauren.

'So, is it a movie or sitting with our feet up in front of the TV?' Lisa asked.

'Won't your mom ask us to help out in the diner

if we stick around?' Kirstie knew the routine; they'd be ten minutes into the TV show and Bonnie would have a rush of customers. Before they knew it, she and Lisa would be dragged down to wait tables.

'Nope.' Lisa's eyes sparkled with a piece of news that she was bursting to share. 'Mom got new help. Take a look.'

So they stepped inside the diner to see Marie North neatly and efficiently setting out the ketchup bottles beside the holly and silver-bauble Christmas arrangements on each table. She wore Lisa's striped apron over black pants and a red checked shirt. With a touch of mascara and lip rouge, she looked ten years younger.

'How come?' Kirstie hissed.

'Mom offered her a job. We need the help over the Christmas period, and Marie sure needs the pay cheque. So they came to an arrangement.'

Studying Lisa's face, Kirstie knew there was more. 'And?' she prompted.

'And we called my grandpa last night. He's snowed in up at the trailer park and won't be using his house in town over the vacation.'

Lennie Goodman, Lisa's grandpa, ran the Lone Elm Trailer Park out beyond Bear Hunt Overlook. It was a remote spot, but since he'd been widowed three years before, the old man was content to spend his winters out there, holed up with provisions, a store of logs and a pile of good books. Which left his home on Main Street vacant for much of the year.

'Don't tell me; you persuaded him to rent his house to the Norths,' Kirstie guessed.

'Right. Actually, Grandpa said not to charge rent. He's more than happy for the house to be used and taken care of. He reckons the Norths are the ones doing him the favour.'

'And Chuck accepted the offer?'

'Sure. But only for a couple of weeks while he finds work and gets back on his feet. Oh, and only if Grandpa lets him fix the floorboards in the porch and put up a new fence. Then it was a fair deal.'

Their minds filled now with the Norths' slowly improving situation, both girls decided to give the movie a miss. They went upstairs to Bonnie and Lisa's apartment, read magazines, tried on clothes, fixed each other's hair.

'How about we mosey along to Grandpa's place,' Lisa dropped in casually, about an hour after Kirstie had arrived. 'We could show Jay and his dad how to use the dishwasher and the tumble-drier.'

'Fascinating!' Kirstie grinned. 'I'm sure they can't

live without knowing how to do laundry!'

But she went along with Lisa's bubbly curiosity, thinking that if anyone could break down Jay North's wall of shyness and overcome the awareness of his terrible illness, then her friend was the one.

'Follow me!' Lisa instructed, checking her unruly hair one last time and marching Kirstie down the stairs. She called into the diner to tell Marie and Bonnie where they were headed, then went out dressed only in her new shirt and jeans – which she wanted to show off – to face the icy wind.

'You gotta suffer to be beautiful,' she joked, her teeth chattering as they approached Lennie's house. 'No pain, no gain!'

Glad of her own thick, lumberjack-style jacket which she wore for her work in the stables, Kirstie smiled. 'I only hope Jay appreciates your sacrifice.'

As Lisa went up the stoop on to the porch and raised her hand to knock on the front door, Chuck North came out to greet them. 'I can't stop,' he explained hurriedly, jamming his well-worn stetson over his forehead. 'I just got a call from the Circle R, asking me to go on over there and talk to Donna Rose about a ranch management position.'

Lisa and Kirstie stepped aside to let him pass.

'Way to go!' Lisa wished the worried man luck in

his search for work. 'Do you mind if we run over a few house items with Jay while you're gone?'

'Go right ahead.' Jumping into an old Dodge pick-up truck parked at the gate, Chuck North set off.

And Lisa and Kirstie entered the homely, old-fashioned house, its walls lined with bookshelves and decorated with the antlers of moose, elk and deer. Battered leather armchairs heaped with cushions created an obstacle course of the downstairs rooms, while brass wall-lamps made pools of yellow light on the brown and black wool rugs.

'Jay?' Lisa called out, having wandered through into the kitchen at the back of the house. 'You there?'

Kirstie heard footsteps coming slowly downstairs. She prepared a smile and turned. 'Hey,' she greeted him, trying not to force the friendliness and to act natural. But it came out awkward anyhow.

Jay scowled back. 'My parents are out,' he told them.

'That's OK. We just wanted to find out if you'd settled in.' Briskly Lisa opened a small closet door to check the settings on the heating system. 'Is there anything you need: extra crockery, knives and forks, that kind of stuff?'

'No.' Jay stonewalled his visitors with an unwavering, suspicious stare. Then he came out with the same kind of ungracious, bitter statement that he'd dumped on Kirstie the day before. 'Listen, you don't need to be nice to me just because I'm ill.'

'We're not . . . that isn't the reason . . .' Even Lisa faltered.

'Yeah, it is. I can see pity in every move you make. And no thanks; I don't need it. Not from you. Not from anyone.'

'OK, OK.' Backing off into the hallway, Lisa's normal confidence gave out. 'Listen, we're sorry . . . not about the leukaemia stuff . . . well, sure we're sorry about that, but that's not what I meant . . .'

Back off, Lisa! Kirstie thought. She knew all too well how it was when you opened your big mouth and put your foot in it.

Jay stared at them, enjoying their discomfort in some weird, twisted way.

I guess if you're angry and scared, that's how you act, Kirstie said to herself. *You make other people feel bad because you hurt like heck inside.* The realisation helped her over her awkwardness. 'Actually, it's not you I feel sorry for right now,' she said, looking Jay in the eye.

'No?' His gaze flickered.

'No. It's that little Polish Arab you dumped on us.' Risky, she knew. But she wanted to goad him into saying how he felt.

'We didn't dump Starlight,' Jay protested. 'Anyways, what were we supposed to do; pack him up in a trunk with the rest of our belongings?'

Kirstie shrugged. 'I have my own horse. He's a palomino called Lucky.'

'So?'

'So, if we had to sell up and move on, no way would I part with him. I'd do anything to keep him; work at a supermarket checkout, do extra chores, just so I could hang on to him. Lucky and me, we belong together.'

'Yeah, but you're not travelling to the hospital every other week for chemotherapy,' Jay pointed out, his eyes showing signs of life at last. 'You don't have parents who worry themselves sick over you.'

'Good point,' Lisa murmured, fearing that Kirstie had been too harsh. She was ready to turn tail and run.

'So?' Either this tactic would work as a piece of inspired thinking on Kirstie's part, or there she was with *both* big feet well and truly stuck in her mouth. 'Does that stop you from visiting Starlight when you're not at the hospital, like now, for instance?'

Wow, was she in it deep!

'Do you suppose I don't want to visit him?' Jay flashed her a look, then strode across her path so that she couldn't follow Lisa to the door. 'Really, is that what you think?'

'So who's stopping you?' This didn't make sense; unless Chuck and Marie North had a hand in it.

Watching Kirstie put two and two together, Jay nodded. 'Right. My parents. They got it into their heads that since I had to part with Starlight, the best thing was to make the break complete. No visits. No phone calls to ask how he was getting along.'

'But that sucks!' Lisa spoke out. 'What would be the harm with you keeping in touch with the horse?'

'Don't ask me. I guess they feel we're handling enough problems as it is, so a clean break is the best. And they made the decision during my last course of therapy, when I was too weak and tired to argue. So that's what I'm stuck with, I guess.'

'Not if you don't want to be.' Kirstie had spotted a tiny glimmer of light at the end of a long, dark tunnel for Jay North and she rushed headlong towards it. 'I could arrange for you to meet up with Starlight if that's what you want.'

'Where? How?' Kirstie's suggestion was like a bolt of energy shooting through him. His whole body shed its lethargy and came alive.

For a moment she thought he was about to grab her by the shoulders and shake the information out of her. 'Would you tell your folks or would it have to be a secret?' she quizzed.

'A secret. Mom and Dad would only try to talk me out of it. So, c'mon, give me the low-down.'

'OK. Can you drive?' Kirstie thought fast. When Jay nodded, she told him to borrow his dad's pick-up and drive out along Route 3 first thing Wednesday morning. 'You take a sign to the left pointing you along the Shelf-Road to Half-Moon Ranch. You can't miss it. OK?'

'Wednesday, Route 3!' Jay took in the information with a rapid nod.

'Two miles before you reach the ranch, you take a fork to the right up a Jeep track signposted Red Eagle Lodge. You drive up the track for another mile, through forest, with Eagle's Peak straight ahead in the distance. After a mile you start looking for a rock on your left shaped like a Christmas angel. Angel Rock.'

More nods, followed by an intense, inquiring look from those energised hazel eyes. 'And you'll be there with Starlight?' he pressed.

Kirstie nodded. 'Nine a.m., Wednesday, unless the weather makes your route impossible. We'll be waiting in the draw under the rock,' she promised faithfully.

4

They stood in the shadow of the angel's wings, sheltering from the wind which blew off the mountain tops.

There'd been snow on Monday, lasting through the night, so that by Tuesday dawn there was a total white-out. Kirstie had looked out at a changed world: no more clean lines of roofs and fence rails, no tracks visible under the fresh fall of snow. The burdened trees had bowed low to the earth; the hillsides were hidden behind a white, powdery mist whipped up by the wind.

And it had been all hands on deck at Half-Moon

Ranch, as Ben, Charlie and Hadley had fixed the snowplough to the front of the tractor and cleared a way out to Red Fox Meadow. Kirstie had watched the metal plough scoop the drifts to one side, leaving giant tyre marks in its wake.

She'd seen the horses struggle and plunge up to their withers to reach the alfalfa hay which the wranglers brought with them, felt a knot of anxiety in her stomach unwind as it became obvious that the tough creatures had set their backs to the snow and wind to make it through the hardest night of the year so far. Soon the snow around the feed-stalls would be trampled flat and the sound of contented munching would remind Sandy and the rest that all was OK.

At eleven-thirty Kirstie had picked up the phone to Jay North.

'Listen, I can't talk long,' he'd gabbled. 'Dad just went out to dig the pick-up out of the snow. Mom's fixing a sandwich in the kitchen. I need to know, did Starlight get through the snowstorm OK?'

Kirstie had reassured him. 'We brought him into the barn midday yesterday. He spent the night indoors and got extra feed this morning. Hadley looks out for the little guy, no problem.'

Jay had given an audible sigh of relief.

'Listen, supposing the Shelf-Road is still blocked tomorrow . . .' Kirstie had begun to make other arrangements for the secret meeting.

'Gotta go. Sorry.' Jay had rung off without waiting for a new plan.

But he'd called again mid-evening. This time Sandy had answered the phone and handed it over to Kirstie with a pleased grin. 'It's your new buddy, Jay.'

Blushing, she'd taken over. 'Hey.'

'About the snow on the Shelf-Road,' he'd started out. 'What do we do if I can't get through?'

'The Forest Rangers are out with their ploughs right now. They already cleared a route from the highway to the point where the Jeep road forks off towards Red Eagle Lodge.' Kirstie had picked up the latest situation on the two-way radios which the ranch hands and the rangers used to communicate with when they were out on the trails. Smiley Gilpin had passed on the message that their ploughs would work through the night and hoped to reach the ranch by Wednesday morning.

'But there'll be a stretch of Jeep road about a mile long between the junction and Angel Rock which won't be cleared,' she'd warned. 'Maybe

Starlight and I should fix to meet you some place else.'

'No, stick with the plan,' Jay had insisted. 'I don't want anyone snooping around, taking the story back to my parents that I went against my word.'

Once more he'd rung off hastily and left Kirstie wondering just how he would make the final mile through the deep drifts to Angel Rock. Most likely on foot; and for a kid who was seriously sick this would be no easy task.

But at least it hadn't snowed any more since Tuesday morning and Wednesday had dawned bright and clear. She'd been able to lead Starlight into the corral and brush and curry him after he'd spent a second night in the barn and eaten at least a small amount of the grain pellets that she'd tipped into his bucket for him.

'You taking the little guy out on the trail?' Hadley had asked in passing.

'Just for a couple of hours,' she'd answered, hoping to escape an inquisition.

The old wrangler had pulled down the corners of his mouth. 'Watch out for drifts,' he'd warned, then unhooked his radio from his belt and handed it over. 'Take this.'

She'd nodded gratefully then saddled up before

anyone else could stop to question her. By eight o'clock she and Starlight were riding out by the frozen creek. By eight forty-five they were in position beneath the angel.

They waited a full thirty minutes.

Starlight's ears were pricked, his tail swishing impatiently. Still in the saddle, Kirstie peered in the direction she knew Jay must take.

'What's keeping him?' she muttered under her breath. Nine-fifteen passed without any sign of a figure struggling on foot along the drifted-up Jeep track.

Starlight stamped his feet and allowed a strong shiver to pass right through his body from head to foot.

'Jeez, maybe his car came off the road!' was her next thought, expressed out loud with a low groan.

The horse picked up her nerviness and began to shift and skit around under her. He sidestepped and pranced, arched his lovely sorrel neck and shook his bridle angrily.

'Easy!' Kirstie said softly. She moved him from under the outspread ledge of rock, down an icy slope and into the shelter of the secluded draw.

It got to nine-thirty and she was fast losing hope,

when Starlight's irritated mood suddenly changed. Instead of stamping and chewing at his bit, he went quiet. Raising his head, he listened.

'What do you hear?' Kirstie whispered, trusting the horse's heightened senses though she herself could pick up nothing but the soft thud of snow as it slid from the laden pines.

Starlight's dark eyes fixed on the white ledge where the angel kept guard. His ears stayed pricked and alert. Not a muscle in his body moved.

Then a thin figure appeared by the rock, stumbling and struggling to the very edge of the ledge.

Jay North.

'We're down here!' Kirstie yelled, finding that her voice was deadened by the snowy surroundings. It took a shrill neigh from Starlight to attract the kid's attention.

Jumping from the saddle and leading the horse by the reins, Kirstie rushed to join up with Jay. 'What kept you? Are you OK?'

He half-slid, half-scrambled down the steep slope into the draw, between two slim aspen trees, towards his horse. 'I had a little accident on the Shelf-Road,' he explained. 'The pick-up came off the track on a bend. I ended up in a ditch.'

'You cut your head!' With a small shock and a shudder, Kirstie noticed a thin trickle of blood from a gash in Jay's temple. It stood out bright scarlet against his pale face.

'It's nothing.' He ignored her concern. With eyes only for Starlight, he made it across the draw.

And Kirstie had enough sense to step right back out of the picture as the two were reunited. She let go of the reins, melted under a tall pine tree and watched in silence.

'Hey, Starlight!' Jay murmured. He stopped a couple of yards from the little Arab, head to one side, taking in every gleaming inch.

The horse trailed his reins along the ground, walking knee-deep through powdery snow right up to Jay. He nuzzled his silky soft nose against his bleeding face.

'How're you doin', buddy?' the boy whispered. He lifted the reins, then unsteadily fondled the horse's neck.

Starlight blew gently through his nostrils, and stood square between Jay and the entrance to the draw, seeming to want to protect him from whatever had caused his injury. He seemed aware too from the boy's breathlessness and lack of balance that he wasn't strong. So he invited him to lean his weight against his shoulder and rest.

'Jeez, I missed you!' Jay breathed, leaning into the sorrel. 'Did you miss me?'

Kirstie withdrew further under the tree, feeling out of place. She was certain by this time that Jay North had entirely forgotten she was there.

'I miss you when I wake up in the morning, right through to when I go to sleep at night,' he went on. 'Then I dream about you and wake up thinking about you all over again. I'm wondering, are you OK? Are they taking care of you? Will I ever get to see you again?'

Starlight turned his beautiful head closer still and breathed warmth over Jay. *Lean on me. Stay with me.*

'It's great to be here with you,' Jay told him softly. 'I feel right now that things are gonna work out; everything's gonna be OK. I'll get my transplant and all that hospital stuff will be over. Then I'll come looking for you and take you home for good!'

Head to head, the horse listened as if he understood every word. Then they stood in silence for minutes on end.

Snow thudded gently. Ice cracked and began to thaw as the sun reached into the draw.

Time to break up the reunion, time to go.

Kirstie stepped out from under the tree.

* * *

That was a moment she would never forget – the look on Jay's face as she went up to them and told them gently that they had to say goodbye.

It was harder than anything she'd done. There were no words to soften it, no way of telling whether or not Jay would ever be well enough to make a return visit to Angel Rock.

The stricken look was what happened to someone when you broke their heart, she knew as she rode Starlight back to the ranch.

Half-startled, turning to panic, there had been a moment's denial as Jay had struggled to put off the moment of parting.

'We have to go. You need to get back to town,' she'd insisted gently.

Jay had let go of Starlight's reins. His hands had dropped to his sides, he'd hung his head.

Goodbye, maybe forever.

Empty. Unresisting. Broken-hearted.

Kirstie never told anyone exactly what had taken place at Angel Rock.

When she summarised it for Lisa on the phone later that day, she simply said that the reunion had been a great success. Both boy and horse had been overjoyed to see each other.

She missed out the part about the tears in Jay's eyes when they said goodbye and the details about Starlight's mournful plod back to Half-Moon Ranch. It was like the spirit had gone out of him; his head was heavy, his legs weary.

Occasionally he would stop, turn and listen. Maybe he heard Jay start the pick-up and head for town more than a mile down the mountain. It was possible; horses' senses were a thousand times better than a human's. If so, he would pay attention to the fading engine as it headed out along the Shelf-Road, listen in vain for Jay to change his mind and return. He would lose hope. Down his head would go and that was when a weary weight had entered his step.

'What do you mean by "a great success"?' Lisa wanted more information. 'Was it really neat to see those two together again?'

'Yeah, cool,' Kirstie replied, doggedly keeping things vague.

'So what now?'

Kirstie held a long silence.

'What happens next?' Lisa insisted.

Zilch. Nothing. Big fat zero.

'Right. OK. Now I guess we wait for the hospital guys to find the right bone marrow match.' Lisa supplied her own answer. 'Once Jay gets well again, we take it from there!'

'That little Polish Arabian is totally off his feed,' Matt reported next morning as Kirstie helped Ben and Charlie clean bridles in the tack-room. 'I tell you, it looks bad. He's not much more than a skeleton already.'

'Maybe we should get him checked over by Glen Woodford next time he calls by,' Ben suggested. 'We could ask him to get on the computer and run through the healthcare programme Starlight received when he was at Mile High Ranch; check out his vaccinations and so on.'

But Matt shook his head. 'I learned enough at vet school to know that's not the problem,' he argued. 'And I already checked to see if he was running a fever. I tell you, there's nothing medically wrong with that horse. It's this place that's all wrong for him.'

'Arabian's don't do well at altitude, do they?' Charlie chipped in.

Ben shrugged. 'Mile High wasn't exactly at sea-level, remember.'

'So what's the answer?' Matt turned to Kirstie, 'More of your TLC, huh?'

'It's not *my* tender loving care he wants,' she replied shortly, throwing her cleaning rag on to the bench. To hide the depth of her concern she had to make a quick exit out into the corral, where she unexpectedly bumped into Bonnie and Lisa.

'Yeah, yeah, don't tell me. It's great to see me,' Lisa said, reacting wryly to the gloomy expression Kirstie wore.

Kirstie managed a faint smile. 'What're you doing all the way out here?'

'Mom wanted to drop in at Grandpa's with some new library books and a few groceries. But we only got as far as Smiley's place before the snowdrifts beat us. Smiley says he'll take the stuff on up as soon as the ploughs make it through to Lone Elm.'

Walking with Kirstie across the corral towards the barn while Bonnie went into the ranch house to have coffee with Sandy, Lisa took the chance to study her friend's troubled looks. 'OK, what's the deal?'

'It's Starlight. He won't eat.' Kirstie led the way into the dark warmth of the barn, past Gulliver and Johnny Mohawk's stalls until they came to the one occupied by the ailing sorrel.

'Jeez.' Lisa took one look. 'How thin is that!'

Starlight stood in the shadows, his white star and pale mane standing out in the gloom. There was just enough daylight to pick out the bars of his rib-cage and the sharp angles of his withers where the flesh had fallen away.

'Thin,' Kirstie sighed. 'And his attitude's all wrong. Look at him; he's just pining away in front of us!'

Lisa thought for a long while. 'Was yesterday a mistake?'

'I didn't think so when we planned it.' But Kirstie had had twenty-four hours to reconsider since the reunion at Angel Rock. 'I just didn't see the bad side of getting Jay and Starlight back together, I guess.'

'Maybe Chuck and Marie were right after all.' Lisa

leaned heavily on the partition separating them from Starlight. She scuffed the toe of her boot against the floor, then came up with yet another unwelcome piece of news. 'Y'know Chuck found out what happened?'

'Jeez, no!' Kirstie gasped. 'How come?'

'According to Marie, Jay gets back from his so-called Christmas shopping trip with a bad gash on his forehead. His dad gives him the third degree: "Did you have a wreck? Where did it happen? Did you drive off-road? Give it to me straight!" Jay finally caves in under the pressure and confesses everything.'

Sucking in more air and clenching her fists, Kirstie held herself together. 'So Chuck North knows I fixed up the reunion?'

Lisa nodded without saying anything.

'Is he mad?'

Another nod. 'Marie tried to tell him that you meant well. And apparently Jay made a big thing of accepting all the responsibility. Anyways, that all kinda fades into the background when I tell you the latest.'

'Which is?'

'The hospital in Denver called as the three of them sat down to supper last night. They said to pack Jay's bag and rush him in fast as they could.'

Wednesday, six days before Christmas, suppertime. A sudden phone call out of the blue. Kirstie pictured the scene. 'Was it the one they've been waiting for?'

Lisa nodded. She spoke quietly, hardly daring to hope, but excited for the Norths nevertheless. 'The doctors say they may have found the right bone marrow match to cure Jay's leukaemia. Isn't that totally fantastic?'

5

'You did what?' Sandy Scott's eyes were filled with consternation. 'Kirstie, are you seriously telling me that you set up a secret meeting between Jay and Starlight?'

More than forty-eight hours had passed since the reunion at Angel Rock, and bigger events had overtaken the Norths. But Kirstie still felt a painful responsibility for what she'd done.

For a start, she only had to look at Starlight to see the effect.

The poor little guy was refusing to touch a scrap of food or even to take a drink from the water bucket in the corner of his stall.

'It ain't natural,' Ben had muttered, looking in on him early Friday morning. And he'd taken it on himself to call in Glen Woodford from the veterinary centre in town.

Matt had come across with his usual grumbles. 'What did I tell you?' he'd muttered. 'I knew that horse was gonna end up costing us money. When's Mom gonna wake up to the fact that we're not running a rest-home for unwanted horses here at Half-Moon?'

'Starlight is *not* unwanted!' Kirstie had retorted fiercely, catching her mother's eye. She'd coloured up and tried to walk away, but Sandy had pursued her into the corral and pressed her to reveal all she knew. 'There's something going on around here that I don't get,' she'd insisted. 'And my hunch is that you, my girl, are dead in the centre of it!'

So Kirstie had confessed about the secret meeting. Her heart had pounded as she described the magic of the moment: the pure snow of the secluded draw, the sun lifting the shadows, the ice sparkling like diamonds.

But then tears had come to her eyes when she told her mom about the parting, and how it had struck her like a kick in the stomach that maybe this whole thing had been a dreadful mistake after all.

And Sandy's reaction now confirmed this impression. 'Kirstie, that was a heck of a thing to take on. Didn't you realise that Chuck and Marie must have had good reasons for keeping Jay and Starlight apart while he goes through his medical programme?'

Kirstie stood miserably in the open, empty corral. There was snow in the air. Heavy, dull clouds were rolling in from the west. 'I'm sorry,' she acknowledged.

Sandy stood, hands on hips, staring up at specks of swirling snowflakes. 'Chuck and Marie figured they could trust us to take care of Starlight and help the family through a bad time.'

'I know.' Somehow – in a way she didn't fully understand – Kirstie had let down an awful lot of people, plus one precious horse. 'What's gonna happen if Glen can't pin down what's wrong with Starlight?' she asked in a faint voice, seeing the vet's black Jeep drive under the Half-Moon Ranch sign at the top of the hill.

Sandy frowned. In her present mood she wasn't ready to let Kirstie off the hook. 'We know what's wrong with the horse,' she said shortly, striding out into the yard to meet the vet. 'He's giving up the will to live. It's called dying of a broken heart!'

'What's the latest news about the North kid?' Ben asked Glen Woodford as the vet ran Starlight through a series of thorough checks.

Jay's illness was the only subject people in San Luis were discussing right now – it had displaced Christmas as the major topic of conversation – and even the next impending snowstorm had taken a back seat as folk concentrated on the medical crisis facing the small family.

'They say the bone marrow donor can provide a perfect match,' Glen reported. 'They still have to do more tests, but Bonnie Goodman's been in touch with Marie North and she says it's looking good.'

'That's great.' Ben gave a quick nod and glanced in Kirstie's direction. 'Looks like your new buddy is in there with a chance.'

Nodding back, Kirstie wished with all her heart that Glen would come up with the same sort of news about Starlight.

'So what's the verdict?' Ben asked, as the vet stashed his stethoscope away in his bag.

Glen stood back from the horse to consider things. He ran his eye up and down Starlight's thin frame, noted the dullness of his coat, the dejected hang of his head, the blankness of his large, dark eyes. 'This has got me beat,' the vet admitted. He was a square, strongly built man with greying hair – not very tall, but tough and solid – the type whose opinion even the most hardbitten ranchers in the Meltwater Range tended to go along with.

'He's not running a fever?' the wrangler quizzed.

'Nope. Temperature's normal. The same with blood pressure, heartbeat, lungs and gut. Everything should be functioning OK. There ain't a thing physically wrong with this guy as far as I can tell.'

Ben allowed an exasperated sigh to escape. 'I saw you taking a blood sample. Will you run tests back at the lab?'

Glen nodded. 'I'll try to get them processed before Christmas, see what we can come up with.'

'But you're not hopeful?' Ben could read into the vet's measured remarks the notion that Starlight's case was coming across as a major medical mystery.

Approaching Starlight once more, Glen ran a broad hand down the horse's neck. 'The problem is, these guys have a pretty primitive digestive system. They can't afford to give up eating for too long. If the nutrition isn't passing through on a consistent basis, all the other organs go into crisis pretty much straightaway: liver, lungs, heart. Before you know it, you have a critically ill animal on your hands.'

'How near to that stage are we with this one?' Ben wanted to know.

Glen stroked Starlight and patted him to draw some response. But the sorrel stayed still and unresponsive. 'Pretty close,' he admitted. 'I'd say we'll be there before we get the blood results; say Monday or Tuesday. That's unless you or Kirstie here can get him to take a little food and plenty of water meanwhile.'

'And can you pin a reason on it?' Ben pressed for as much information as the vet could give him.

Glen hesitated. 'I'm a plain old veterinarian, not one of these fancy animal psychologists you get out on the West Coast. Who can tell what really goes on in a horse's mind?'

'But it's likely to be psychological?' Ben frowned more deeply than before.

'Look at it this way. Like I say, I'm no expert, but a horse like this spends all his time growing up with one kid. Starlight looks on Jay North as a prime member of his family; or if you like, Jay's the herd leader and Starlight depends on him to be told what to do.

'So when the break comes, it leaves the horse in limbo. All his normal support systems are gone. He comes here to Half-Moon Ranch; he doesn't know the territory and you can bet your bottom dollar that there aren't too many friendly faces out there in the ramuda.'

True, Kirstie thought. All too horribly accurate.

'Worst of all, he's lost his alpha herd member. Think of his brain as a map. When they separated Starlight from Jay it was like the whole map suddenly went scrambled and meaningless.'

'So he's confused?' Kirstie followed the vet's explanation carefully. 'He needs a new leader.'

'Yeah and no. Like, he can't switch allegiance. He's stuck on Jay. And Jay suddenly isn't here. So what does he do in all this confusion? He says, "OK, I don't get any of this, and I guess I'm just not smart enough to make it alone." So his spirit's broke and he kinda gives in.'

'What happened to his survival mechanism?' Ben wondered. 'Don't all animals have this terrific will to go on living?'

'You'd think,' Glen agreed. 'That's the bit we don't understand. How come, in a case like this, the instinct to survive is overcome by something stronger?'

'By a broken heart, for instance?' Kirstie whispered.

She saw it all clearly; it all made perfect sense. Her mum had been right, and unless they could think of something to do real fast, Starlight wouldn't even live until Christmas.

Snow fell on Friday night; a couple of inches to cover the dirty tyre marks on the roads and make over the scene, back to Christmas-card prettiness. But not enough to hold up the business of the ranch.

Kirstie was up early on the Saturday morning, clattering about in the barn, letting the select band of Breakfast Club horses know she was around.

'Hold it!' she called to little Gulliver, who poked his head eagerly over the nearby stall. 'Just let me cut through the twine on this hay bale, then you can have as much as you can eat!'

The eager palomino colt swayed his head and stamped his feet.

'You hear that, Starlight?' Deliberately upbeat, bustling here and there with armfuls of sweet-smelling hay, Kirstie tried to let him know that life went on as usual. 'Gulliver's hungry. He'll eat up your portion if you let him!'

Hoping for a response, but getting none, she decided to go into the sorrel's stall and offer him hay from her palm. 'Just a little,' she encouraged.

Starlight sniffed at the alfalfa and turned away. In the grey, cold light of dawn, he gave off the same listless, dejected lack of interest as ever.

'Y'know, there's no real reason for you to be moping around like this.' Fussing him, even scooping a handful of water from the bucket to tempt him to drink, now was a time if ever there was one when Kirstie wished that a horse had the power to understand human speech. 'Jay's in the hospital in Denver, getting the treatment he needs. For all we know, he'll be out in a week or two, and then he can come visit. I'm sure his parents will allow it once they hear how sick you've gotten without him.'

The shivering horse heaved a deep sigh, rejecting the water and sidling away to the far corner of the stall.

'Hey, and things are looking up for the whole family. They have a nice place to stay in town, and Chuck may get himself a position on Donna Rose's ranch, who knows? Think about that, Starlight. A new beginning for Jay, Chuck and Marie out at the

Circle R. And Donna's a real nice lady. What's the betting she'd eventually find space on the ranch for a pretty Polish Arabian like you?'

This was stretching it, maybe, but it was the kind of outcome that every single person who knew the Norths' story would wish for.

And now, after all her cajoling and coaxing him to come back and join the world, Starlight was in fact beginning to pay Kirstie some attention.

Maybe it was the quiet dawn-time, maybe the soothing sound of her voice and the soft feel of her hands as she stroked and petted him. In any case, he turned his head as she began work with a soft brush, whisking away stray wisps of straw from his curved back, working at his flanks and thin belly.

'Does this feel good?' she murmured. 'Is it the way Jay used to do it?'

Starlight snorted. As he drew breath, his ribcage moved sharply in and out, then relaxed into a more even and contented rhythm.

Kirstie brushed on as the first rays of wintry sunlight slanted into the barn. She grew warm with the work, stopping to take off her checkered jacket and roll up her sweatshirt sleeves. While she paused, Starlight took it into his head to wander over to the water bucket and take a few cautious sips.

'Good boy!' Kirstie praised him. 'You need to keep on drinking plenty to stop you getting weaker. Now how about some of this sweet hay?'

The horse stopped sucking up liquid and raised his head. His wide nostrils flared as he came across to sniff at the alfalfa. Then he curled back his upper lip to expose his teeth and nipped a small mouthful from her palm.

'Cool!' she breathed. 'Boy, do I love the sound of those teeth crunching away!'

Starlight chewed, swallowed and took another few strands, eating at last because he seemed willing to please Kirstie rather than out of his own hunger.

'Like, "*If this is what she wants me to do, I may as well put a smile on her face*"!' Kirstie described the scene to Lisa on the phone later that morning. 'Believe me, that's a real people-horse; the type that would go to the ends of the earth and use every last breath for you!'

'You sound good,' Lisa commented.

'I feel mighty relieved,' she confessed. Four times during the morning she'd approached Starlight with small quantities of hay. On each occasion he'd tried to please her by nibbling a few mouthfuls. And the level in the water bucket was way down, showing that he was drinking plenty.

'If he pulls through, you know it's down to you. I can't think of anybody else who could break through that kind of barrier and set up a new bond with the poor guy.'

'It's the least I could do after Angel Rock,' Kirstie told her. 'Starlight's not out of danger yet, I guess. Glen Woodford hasn't gotten back to us yet with the blood test results; they'll show up any damage to his internal organs that might have occurred over these few days of starving himself. But these last twelve hours sure make things look better. I reckon all Starlight has to do is keep on the way he's going now and hold out until Jay gets out of the hospital and comes to visit.'

'I'm glad.'

'Hey, how come you're so quiet?' Suddenly Kirstie realised that Lisa wasn't fizzing with energy on the other end of the phone.

'Well, to tell you the truth, things aren't so good this end.'

'Why, what happened?'

'It's Jay as a matter of fact. You know they found a match and we thought that solved the problem? Well, it's not so simple.'

'How come? Why can't they go ahead and do the transplant?'

Lisa explained as best she could. 'I'm not exactly sure. It's something to do with Jay's blood count. White and red blood cells; that kind of stuff. Whatever. The doctors have had to give him a major blood transfusion and wait for the count to come good before they can go ahead with the transplant. Marie says it could take a few more days; maybe until after Christmas.'

The setback took some of the wind out of Kirstie's sails. 'I guess we'll all have to hang on in,' she said quietly. Then, 'Listen, Lisa, you pass on the good news about Starlight. Let Jay know that he's doing OK now.'

'Sure,' came the promise. 'Mom and I plan to visit the hospital tomorrow. I'll tell him then.'

Kirstie woke next morning long before daybreak. She lay in bed listening to the wind whistling through the pine trees at the back of the house, wondering exactly what it was that had woken her.

Was it the dream she'd been having that had disturbed her sleep? Something about doctors in surgical gowns, crowding around, then floating off. And Kirstie had been the patient, half anaesthetised and trying to explain that it wasn't her who was ill . . .

Or was it something outside? A car engine breaking in through the moaning wind, a door slamming . . .

She sat up in bed. That really was a car door being closed in the yard.

Scrambling into her clothes, she was downstairs before anyone else in the house was alert to their unexpected visitor, and out in the porch holding a flashlight, fixing the figure of Chuck North in its yellow beam.

'For God's sake, you've gotta help us!' he cried when he spotted her. Behind him, Marie North struggled out of a car Kirstie recognised as belonging to Bonnie Goodman. Both of Jay's parents looked devastated by some unknown crisis, and what Chuck was saying wasn't making any sense to her slow brain.

'Is he here? Do you know where he is? C'mon, answer me!' The frantic man put up his hand to stop the glare from the flashlight. He rushed on to the porch, pushing past into the house.

'Do you mean Jay? Isn't he in the hospital?' Confusion made Kirstie step out into the snow-covered yard in her bare feet to intercept Marie North.

'No. He only went and discharged himself!' Marie

cried, her face drained. 'God knows what he was thinking. He just walked out in the middle of the night while his father and I were asleep in one of the hospital family rooms. He jumped right into the pick-up and drove off before anyone had chance to stop him!'

Kirstie gasped. 'Why would he do that?'

Chuck North burst back out of the house. 'Because he was worried sick about his darned horse, that's why!'

'Chuck, please . . . !' Trying to restrain her husband from rushing mindlessly here and there, Marie tried to explain. 'Starlight has been the only thing Jay could think about ever since Wednesday morning. He's convinced the horse is pining away without him. And when the doctors told him they had to put off the transplant for a few days, he nearly went crazy, begging them to let him out, telling his father and me that he didn't care what happened to him; Starlight was the only thing that mattered.'

Kirstie felt the breath squeezed from her body as she realised what was happening. No wonder, when Jay's parents had been woken up in the middle of the night to be told about his disappearance, their first thought had been to get out here to Half-Moon Ranch.

By this time, lights were going on all over the house and out in the bunkhouse where Ben and Charlie slept.

'You stay here!' Kirstie gasped to Marie. 'Tell my mom what you just told me.'

'What about you?'

She pointed to the figure of Chuck North. He was running across the yard, vaulting the fence into the corral, racing on towards the closed door of the barn. 'I'll follow your husband!' she yelled, setting off still barefoot, hair whipped across her face by the wind, feeling cold flakes on her cheeks. 'Send the others after us fast as you can!'

6

Kirstie knew with chilling certainty that the horse would be gone.

Chuck North's yell of frustration as he ran ahead to the stall and discovered the open door, the scattered straw and the lead-rope and headcollar hanging loose from a hook in the wall only confirmed her fears.

Joining him, she shone her flashlight into the empty stable.

'This is crazy!' Chuck groaned, allowing himself to sag forward against the swinging door, as if the sudden disappointment had knocked the breath out of him. 'What in the world does Jay figure all this is doing to his mom and me?'

'I guess he's not thinking straight.' Kirstie tried to put herself in Jay's place. Hospital must have seemed like a prison to him, and the news that he had to wait for his transplant must have come as the final straw. There, at the forefront of his mind, completely displacing his mom and dad's desperate worry on his account, before even the dangers of his own situation, was the image of Starlight.

Starlight standing in the snow in the shadow of Angel Rock. Starlight pining away on a mountain ranch, living among strangers.

The knowledge must have gnawed away inside Jay's head during the long minutes and hours ticking by on the hospital wall-clock.

So he'd waited until the dead of night, until the nurse on duty had tucked herself away behind her station to fill in charts and enter information on to the computer. Then he'd snuck out, down long, empty corridors, through the sliding doors into the parking lot. He'd jumped into the family pick-up and raced out along the neon-lined Interstate into the blackness of mountainous country roads, driving recklessly along the frozen Shelf-Road to reach Half-Moon Ranch before the alert was raised back at the hospital.

And he'd made it in one piece, dumping the pick-up somewhere out of sight, heading straight for the barn where his beloved horse would be alert and waiting . . .

'Crazy!' Chuck muttered again. 'Doesn't he know he could freeze to death out there?'

'I don't reckon they can have been gone long.' Thinking fast, Kirstie was all set to run for the tack-room to see if Starlight's saddle and bridle were also missing.

But as she reached the barn door, she bumped headlong into Bonnie and Lisa, who, it turned out, had come running down from the cattle-guard at the top of the hill.

'We found the pick-up!' Lisa gasped. 'Jay must've dumped it at the ranch entrance and snuck down on foot!'

'What are you doing here?' Kirstie demanded. For a moment she hadn't recognised the dark, muffled figures.

'Chuck and Marie headed all the way out of Denver to our place in a taxi cab before we drove them out here.' Lisa's explanation was hurried. Behind her the activity inside the ranch house was increasing. By now, Matt had emerged on to the porch and was trying hard to calm Marie North. 'They reckoned there was a chance that Jay had stopped off at Grandpa's house for warm clothes, since it's on the way to the ranch. They say he can only be wearing jeans and a light jacket; no way is he dressed for this kind of weather!'

Kirstie nodded. 'OK, so there was no sign of Jay stopping off in San Luis; they checked with you to be double-sure?'

'Right. Mom and I woke up in the middle of the night to a phone call from Marie, speaking from Grandpa's place. We knew straightaway it must be an emergency.'

'So you jumped into your car and drove them the rest of the way.' Kirstie got the picture.

'Yep. When we reached here, I saw tyre marks in the snow, leading off up a trail to the side of the cattle-guard. So Mom and I got out of the car to check it out, while Chuck and Marie drove on down to the house.'

'And the tyre tracks led you to the pick-up, like you figured?' So far, it seemed that Jay's movements had been totally predictable because of the fixation he had for Starlight. From now on, though, his actions might prove more difficult to second-guess.

Where would a sick kid with an ailing horse ride in the middle of the night in the dead of winter at an altitude of ten thousand feet?

'Come with me!' Kirstie told Lisa, as Bonnie went off to join the adults gathering in the porch.

The girls headed for the tack-room in the half-light, to discover the door open and Starlight's saddle missing.

'That settles it,' Lisa muttered as Cornbread the tack-room cat glided silently between the saddle-racks.

She and Kirstie went out again to report their finding and to discover the next move.

'I say we bring in the cops right away,' Chuck North was insisting, rejecting Matt's more cautious idea that they should hold off until daybreak and then form a search-party of their own. 'Why wait? Every minute that passes means our son is getting himself into deeper trouble!'

'But I don't see what it has to do with the cops,' Matt pointed out. 'What's the crime here exactly?'

'OK, so we call in the Forest Guard instead!' Chuck switched tack. 'They have Jeeps and radios. They know the territory like the backs of their hands!'

Matt checked with Ben, who had recently arrived

on the porch from his bunkhouse. The wrangler nodded and went away to set in motion this part of the plan.

'And, Ben; contact the Mountain Rescue Team in San Luis,' Matt called after him. 'Ask them if they can stand by with a chopper in case we need it!'

'We're assuming here that Jay and Starlight got clean away from the ranch,' Sandy pointed out. She'd arrived on the porch and succeeded in calming down Marie. As usual her input was steady and considered. 'But we're gonna look pretty foolish if we call in Smiley and the Forest Guard, then we find the two runaways hiding quietly in the trees up by the cattle-guard, say.'

Matt agreed. Quickly he sent Charlie off in the ranch pick-up to scout around all the more obvious places nearby. That left himself and Hadley to check on foot in Red Fox Meadow and along Five Mile Creek.

By now there was a glimmer of light creeping into the horizon and the sound of high, thin birdsong from the frozen trees. Kirstie hovered at the edge of the porch with Lisa, feeling the sharp edge of the cold wind cut right through her.

'Go get some socks and boots on,' Sandy ordered.

'If you want to be any help here, you need to be fully dressed.'

Kirstie rushed inside the house to do as she was told, shoving her numb feet into woollen socks and struggling into her tough leather boots.

'What do we do?' Lisa followed and pressed her impatiently for their next move. 'How come all the guys have got a job to do and we don't?'

'I guess we do our own thing.' Kirstie's idea was that she and Lisa should backtrack to the barn and try to identify Starlight's prints in the snow. 'That way, at least we pick up clues to tell us which way they headed,' she explained. 'And with luck, we'll be able to follow the prints for a good way, out along one of the trails.'

Lisa frowned. 'The snow's pretty trampled and messy out there. Picking out one set of prints ain't gonna be easy.'

'I didn't say it would be *easy*!' Snapping back, Kirstie's look challenged Lisa to come up with a better idea. Then she backed down. 'Sorry. I guess this is getting to me worse than I thought.'

They went out on to the porch together, to find the Norths still deep in conversation with Bonnie and Sandy.

'You wanna know the worst thing about all this?'

Marie struggled hard to hold back the tears as Chuck stood with his arm around her shoulder. 'The nurse on night duty at the hospital had just been recording Jay's latest blood count on to his file. The update showed that it had improved enough for them to go ahead with the transplant sooner than they thought.'

'Tomorrow maybe,' Chuck added resentfully. 'It could all have been through by Christmas after all. But Jay didn't stick around long enough to find out.'

'That's tough,' Bonnie agreed.

'Yeah, and we didn't get chance to tell him the good news about Starlight starting to eat and drink a little,' Lisa added guiltily. 'I guess if he'd known about that, he wouldn't have been so desperate to make a run for it.'

Her mention of the horse attracted Chuck's attention to the girls. 'You and the stupid horse!' he accused Kirstie in a bitter tone. 'If you hadn't taken it into your head to set up that meeting, no way would Jay have grown so fixated. This would all have worked out a whole lot different!'

The jibe cut Kirstie to the core. Even though she knew that Chuck North wasn't normally the type to hold a grudge or go around laying blame, she could see there might be some truth in his accusation. So she hung her head and bit her lip, unable to offer excuses.

'I reckon you should back off a little,' Lisa said for her. 'When you stop to think about it, there's no way of knowing if the thing at Angel Rock made Jay feel worse or better. Maybe it helped get him through a few more days of waiting for his treatment. Maybe if he hadn't seen Starlight last Wednesday, he'd have reached breaking-point earlier.'

Marie was gracious enough to acknowledge that Lisa might be right. 'Anyways, there's no point wondering. What we need to do is find Jay and Starlight before anything real bad happens.'

'There are plenty of us out looking,' Sandy reminded her. She glanced out across the yard as Ben came back from making his calls to Smiley Gilpin at Red Eagle Lodge and to the twenty-four-hour rescue service in town.

'Smiley's raising three Jeeps, each with a two-man crew,' the wrangler reported. 'But Ricky Thornton reckons he can't send us a helicopter until he finds out more about a severe weather warning that just came out from the meteorological office in Colorado Springs.'

'What kind of severe weather?' Sandy asked,

studying the slowly lightening horizon. She noted clouds settled all along the jagged skyline and recognised without being told that at these sub-zero temperatures the heavy, blue-black clouds denoted a lot more snow.

'Gale force winds from the west.' Ben gave the details. 'Up to ninety miles per hour in this neck of the woods. On top of that, the met. guys forecast at least six inches of snowfall.'

Sandy listened then acted decisively. 'OK, we need to let Matt and the others know about that. It's gonna affect what we can safely do from here.'

'How soon do the wind and snow reach us?' Chuck wondered.

'In two, maybe three hours,' Ben told him. 'Yeah, I know; that doesn't give us long to track down Jay, so we'd best get a move on.'

Then it was all action, with Sandy suggesting to Bonnie, Chuck and Marie that they jump into her car and that she drive them out along the Jeep road which stopped a mile or so short of Angel Rock. 'My best guess is that Jay will have ridden Starlight out to a place he knows – one which holds a happy memory for them both. If I'm right, we'll have to dump the car and hike the last stretch to the rock, but if we move fast, there'll be time to get out there and take a good look before the snow hits.'

Which left Ben to man the radio and keep in touch with both Smiley Gilpin and Ricky Thornton in an attempt to coordinate the various arms of the rescue mission. 'Did everyone remember their two-way radios?' he yelled to Sandy as she and her group set off for Angel Rock.

'We got ours,' she replied. 'Make sure that the guys all pick one up before they set out further afield. We don't want anyone running the risk of getting stranded in the mountains without some means of communication!'

Two to three hours; the time scale really put the pressure on, Kirstie knew. So, as the adults dispersed and daylight filtered through the heavy clouds, she led Lisa to the barn where they began to search hard for prints they could identify as belonging to Starlight.

'How will we know which are his?' Lisa muttered, staring helplessly at the jumble of scuffs and marks in the dirty snow.

Kirstie knitted her brows and squatted down for a closer look. 'Luckily Starlight's prints are pretty distinctive,' she explained. 'For a start, he's a small horse with little hooves, so we're looking for undersized shoes. Second, all our normal horses are cold-shoed by a farrier from Mineville, whereas I noticed that the Norths had spent money on having Starlight hot-shoed, which means the farrier could shape the iron more neatly and take more pride in the work. I guess I can spot the difference in a print between an expensive hot-shoed horse and a workaday trail horse.'

'Jeez, I'm impressed!' Careful not to muss up the snow any more by treading over the surface by the main door, Lisa went scouting further afield. 'Y'know, I reckon Jay would have to be pretty dumb to take Starlight up to Angel Rock,' she yelled from a distance as she headed for the barn's side door. 'Like, it's the first place anyone would think of. He'd almost have to want to be found if he took him out there.'

Kirstie nodded in agreement. Despite her confidence on the topic of hot and cold shoes, she was having trouble picking up any single clear print from the trampled mess of human and equine footprints. And if she wasn't mistaken, the threatened gale-force wind was already picking up, bringing with it the arctic smell of the high mountains and cutting through her layers of clothes to make her teeth chatter uncontrollably.

She was about to give in and think again, when

Lisa suddenly shouted from beside the side of the barn.

'Kirstie, come over here, tell me what you make of this.'

'What?' She scrambled around the corner to see a single set of clear prints leaving the barn and heading off around the back in the direction of Five Mile Creek.

'Are these hot shoes or cold shoes?' Lisa wanted to know.

'Hot.' Definitely. Neat, expensive, trailing right along the side of the frozen stream as far as she could see.

'C'mon, what are we waiting for?' Lisa cried.

Kirstie glanced back at the empty yard. 'Maybe we should let Ben know what we found and grab a radio to keep in contact . . .'

'No time!' Lisa insisted. She was already running knee-deep through untrodden drifts, parallel to the tracks made by Starlight, convinced that Jay and his horse were just out of sight behind the nearest tree, or around the very next bend.

So, against her better judgment, Kirstie went after her friend, out into a vast white wilderness of ice and snow.

7

The wind was the big problem.

Without it, Starlight's tracks would've stayed clear and easy to follow, and Kirstie and Lisa's progress along the side of Five Mile Creek would've been faster.

As it was, the gusts whipped up the surface of the recently fallen snow. They swirled clouds of snow across the girls' path and whipped the evidence of the horse's presence clean away from beneath their feet. Then the wind grew stronger and battered against them, so that at times they were forced to take refuge in the lee of a rock and pause to catch their breath before they set out again to search for the vital and fast-disappearing hoofprints.

'Jeez, this is harder than I thought!' Sheltering behind a ten-foot boulder lodged on the bank of the creek, Lisa gasped and shook snow from the brim of her hat.

'Let's hope that Jay and Starlight managed to get out of this wind,' Kirstie muttered. She glanced up anxiously at the heavy clouds, praying that the meteorological guys had been right about the two-hour time lapse before the next snowstorm was due to hit.

'Say they had to take shelter,' Lisa surmised. 'That means they must still be pretty close. In other words, maybe we're not so far behind them.'

The thought made them emerge from behind their boulder and scan the way ahead. They spotted faint hoofprints swerve unsteadily through a stand of bare willow bushes, then crunch unexpectedly into the ice at the edge of the creek.

'Look, they made it through the willows, then crossed the creek!' Kirstie pointed to the cracked surface and showed Lisa where the prints began again on the opposite bank. It was obvious from the scuffed and churned-up surface that Starlight had had a hard time making it up the steep slope.

'Uh-oh, it looks like we're gonna get our feet wet!' Lisa moaned, hesitating for only a moment before she plunged out into the wind once more.

'Wait; maybe the ice will take our weight.' Instead of following the horse's exact path, Kirstie picked her way down one bank on to the ice. As she stepped on to it, she heard it crack and saw the water bubble to the surface. For a moment she thought her foot would go through after all. But no; the layer of ice was thick and strong enough to bear her and she edged across without mishap.

Lisa observed with bated breath. 'OK, now watch me. I'm ten pounds heavier than you, so knowing my luck, this is where I end up with my boots full of ice-cold water!'

But she too took a careful route across the creek, sliding a little on the ice and throwing out both arms to keep her balance. And Kirstie, safe on the far bank, reached out to catch her, easing her on to solid ground then hauling her up the slope.

'Thanks!' Lisa grinned. There was a determined light in her green eyes in spite of the tough conditions they faced.

Kirstie too was growing more hopeful. She found that this bank of the stream was less in the wind and that the snow hadn't drifted so dramatically. So it was possible to follow Starlight's prints away from the creek, up the slope which would lead past Whiskey Rock and eventually to Bear Hunt Trail.

'It's what we thought: no way did Jay head for Angel Rock,' she commented, realising that her mom, Bonnie, Chuck and Marie were heading in precisely the wrong direction. Also, that those who were searching for the runaways on foot close to the ranch were on an equally false track.

'So, d'you reckon he knows where he's going?' Lisa asked, using handholds to pull herself up away from the creek bed.

'Nope, but I reckon Starlight has his bearings OK,' Kirstie predicted, knowing that it was vital for a horse to recognise and remember landmarks. She followed the trail on to a ridge, to a spot where a tall pine tree had crashed down across the track during a previous storm, presenting a three-foot high, solid barrier of trunk and sprawling roots.

Discovering that Jay and Starlight had back-tracked at this point, they themselves doubled back and followed the prints down a steep slope to the other side of the ridge.

Kirstie frowned. 'Not so good.'

'Because they're off the trail?'

'Yeah. Bushwhacking across country is not what I'd recommend in these conditions,' she confirmed. 'Especially when you recall that Starlight isn't as sure-footed as some of the quarter-horses we have in our string. I'm just worried that he'll put a foot into a hollow or catch his leg against a snarled-up, low branch. Then what?'

'Don't even think about it!' Lisa told Kirstie. She was having enough trouble just standing upright and following the tracks.

Beyond the ridge, the force of the wind had picked up again. It tugged at their clothes and made them lean into it, slowing them down to snail's pace and whipping up the surface of the snow once more.

'I can't see a thing!' Kirstie complained. She tried to look around to fix a landmark in her sights – a familiar rock on the horizon or a trail that might be still visible between snowdrifts. But the landscape seemed strange, hidden beneath new contours, cloaked in white and entirely unrecognisable.

And besides, there was freezing snow blowing directly into her face, forcing her to narrow her eyes to thin slits and duck her head so that she missed her footing and found herself sliding rapidly down a ten-foot stretch of steep hillside until she jammed up against another fallen tree.

'You OK?' Lisa asked, scrambling after her.

'Great!' Struggling out from the gap between the horizontal trunk and the ground, Kirstie shook snow out of every crease and crevice. She took off her leather gloves, which were by this time soaked through, shook the lumps of snow out of them and pulled them back over her freezing fingers.

'You wanna turn back?' Lisa checked uncertainly.

'Yes, I *want* to!' Who in their right mind wouldn't? But the runaways were still out here somewhere. Kirstie looked her friend right in the eye, face to face in a white whirlwind of drifting snow. 'But I guess we can't do that. As long as Jay and Starlight stay missing, we have to press on.'

Wind continued, and then came the snow.

The met. guys were wrong. The fresh storm didn't hold off for two hours. It started less than an hour after Kirstie and Lisa had set off on their search.

The flakes descended slowly at first – white, whirling specks from a leaden grey sky. The wind caught them and gusted them through the tree branches, sticking them to the rough bark of the ponderosa pines and into vertical crevices of the granite rocks all around.

Big snowflakes, perfectly formed. Each one a delicate network of tiny ice crystals, falling in hordes, destroying what little remained of Starlight's tracks.

'Which way now?' Lisa would steady herself against a tree trunk and turn to Kirstie for advice.

Kirstie would search every foot of the way ahead, thinking that perhaps she could still see a hoofprint. 'This way!'

She would advance a few yards, plunge waist-deep into a drift, then realise that she was mistaken after all.

Then they would turn round, start off in a new direction, climb to a vantage point, look out over yet more frozen forest, more valleys and ridges that they seemed never to have seen before.

'What d'you reckon; do we know where we are?' Lisa said after fifteen minutes of battling through the worsening storm.

Silently Kirstie shook her head.

'And we lost Starlight's trail?'

'Way back,' she admitted.

No radio, no supplies, no idea which direction was home.

'Jeez!' was all Lisa said.

The wind had eased, but the snow came down thick, beautiful and deadly. It lay inches deep on the overhead branches, softened every jagged rock, hid each narrow crevice and filled the wide crevasses.

What next? 'Maybe we should head down into the valley,' was Kirstie's first thought. 'If we hit white water rushing through there, the chances are that would be rapids on Shady River. Then we would head downstream until we recognised some place like Marshy Meadows.'

'What if we don't hit the river?' Lisa's teeth chattered as she tried to cower deeper into the thick grey fleece jacket she was wearing over a black turtle-neck sweater. 'Then we're in deep trouble, huh?'

'OK, so maybe we climb back on to that ridge.' Kirstie turned the way they'd come. 'If we go high, we should get a long view. Then maybe we can pick out a landmark or two.'

Agreeing that this was a better idea, Lisa let Kirstie lead the way. 'Hold it, don't get too far ahead!' she warned, falling behind as she lost her balance and slid sideways into an unseen dip.

Kirstie glanced back over her shoulder, scared to

realise that although she was only a couple of yards ahead, she could only see Lisa as a faint, shadowy shape through the whirling snow. How easy would it be to lose somebody in conditions like this! And how quick would a person freeze to death if they injured themselves out here and had to cope alone!

The idea jarred her attention back on to the missing Jay and Starlight.

'I hope that horse stays on his feet,' she muttered, not even realising that she'd spoken out loud as she returned to lend a hand.

'Did we give up on the search?' Lisa wanted to know, her face pinched and a little scared by now.

Kirstie nodded. 'I don't think we had a choice, did we?'

Somehow this whole thing had turned around. Instead of the heroes who had set out alone to rescue the sick boy and horse, they were likely to return as victims of the wind and snow themselves. That was if they managed to return at all.

She shook herself and slogged on up the slope, bowing her head to shield her face with the brim of her stetson. She was cold through and through, her feet and hands were numb, her brain racing and whirling like the snowflakes all around.

'How long does it take people to die out here?'

Lisa faltered. She'd heard stories, read reports in the newspapers of groups who had been caught in a winter storm, got lost and ended up as fatalities. Their corpses would be dug out of the snow or would end up in Shady River months later as part of the snowmelt off of the tops of the mountains.

Almost at the top of the ridge, Kirstie turned on her. 'Will you stop asking stupid questions and concentrate on finding out where we are!'

'Yeah, sorry.'

They climbed on in silence until they crested the ridge, where they discovered a slight break in the snowfall and a blurred, full 360 degree view of the territory all around.

'Yes!' Kirstie breathed in deep. She pointed to a weird, tall finger of rock standing out on the horizon. 'That's Monument Rock, which makes this ridge we're standing on Bear Hunt Overlook.'

Lisa nodded. 'OK, so that peak to the left of Monument Rock must be Tigawon Mount.' She too knew the area they were gazing towards. 'Which puts Lone Elm Trailer Park about a mile below that weird, humped part of the mountain.'

'What d'you reckon; we head for your grandpa's place?' Better that than plunging back in the other direction for the ranch, which would mean a lot more struggling through draws and valleys without any clear landmark to guide them.

Once they reached Lone Elm, they would be able to meet up with Lennie Goodman and get him to telephone Half-Moon Ranch to pass on the news that she and Lisa were safe.

Without replying out loud, Lisa struck out along the new ridge. 'I guess this is a three-mile hike, which in these conditions will take us two hours plus,' she judged. 'Goddammit, why didn't we do what Ben said and bring a radio with us!'

'Because we were hotheads.' Kirstie too realised that the folks back at the ranch would now be worried sick not only about Jay, but about her and Lisa as well.

By this time her mom and the others would've reached Angel Rock, realised they were on a wild goose chase and hightailed it back home. Charlie would've reported that there was nothing to be seen in any of the obvious nearby places. And Matt and Hadley would've returned empty-handed from the creek. Meanwhile, Ben would be receiving reports of the worsening weather conditions via the radio, which would mean no helicopter from San Luis and an even harder time for Smiley Gilpin and his rangers out in their Jeeps.

Worse and worse, she thought. *Two days before Christmas and three lives at risk. Four, including Starlight.*

'Let's try and make it to Lone Elm real fast,' Lisa murmured, obviously thinking along the same lines.

So they slogged on, often knee-deep in snow, almost used now to the flakes which blinded them and melted on their eyelashes, to the freezing trickles of water down their cheeks and to the knife-sharp coldness of the icy wind.

'Keep Monument Rock in sight!' Lisa gasped, clinging on to their one and only landmark.

'Yeah, like how, when it keeps vanishing behind the clouds?' Struggling along Bear Hunt Overlook was difficult enough, without keeping the rock fixed in view. There were hazards every step of the way: patches of ice hidden by snowdrifts where tiny creeks had frozen across the track, sudden steep falls where the rock had eroded, or branches so heavy with snow that they bent to the earth and blocked the path. 'At least we won't meet a bear on Bear Hunt Overlook,' she grunted, slipping underneath a slanting tree trunk and coming out the far side.

'Yeah, all self-respecting bears are deep in hibernation right now!' Lisa managed to smile.

But it was only for a moment, as the clouds closed in and the blizzard thickened again.

For a while they had to hope for the best and continue along the ridge in what they hoped was the right direction.

'Is this wind getting worse, or what?' Lisa muttered, as a gust practically lifted her off her feet. Overhead, tree branches creaked, and to their right one cracked, broke and went crashing down the slope. They saw the whole tree shudder and a ton of snow come thudding down to the ground.

The storm went on, and if possible grew worse. As Lisa and Kirstie fought their way towards the trailer park, visibility often dropped to a mere five yards. Then it would lift a little to let them see the trail again, and even occasionally give them a glimpse of Monument Rock.

'We're getting there!' Kirstie mumbled, her face almost too frozen to speak. She reckoned another mile would do it, to judge by the line of overhead cables she had just spotted strung out across the mountainside.

This was another clear landmark – the place where the cable riggers had been able to mount a line of giant steel frames on rock ledges which they'd blasted out of the hillside. Then they'd slung the electricity cables between the tall frames, so that they festooned the forest, soaring above the treetops and marked out from time to time with huge orange plastic spheres which hung as markers for low-flying aircraft.

Only, today Kirstie could see that the orange balls were weighted down with snow, dragging the cables dangerously close to the tops of the trees. The cables themselves seemed to sag and stretch and even the steel framework of the fifty-foot-high rigs supporting them looked unstable in the high wind.

'Do we have to pass underneath?' Lisa queried.

'Unless we can grow wings and fly over.' Frowning up at the swaying cables, Kirstie knew there was nothing for it but to take the risk and nip under. Beyond the cables it would be downhill on the final stretch to Lone Elm.

Still Lisa hesitated. 'I don't like the look of it. See how close this nearest stretch of cable is to the trees.'

They both watched as the high-voltage wires sagged and swayed.

And they were concentrating so hard that they seemed to miss the high creak and groan of one of the highest giant pines in a sudden strong blast of wind. The force of the gust was so great that it tore at the ancient roots of the tree, which, made

top-heavy by its snow-laden branches, began to topple forwards towards the girls.

'Watch out!' Kirstie cried as she heard the twisted roots rip from the ground and the telltale thud of snow sliding from the branches.

There was another almighty creak, a crack and an ear-splitting tearing of wood.

All over the forest floor, unseen, hibernating creatures woke with a start, squealed and scurried away from the danger of the suddenly uprooted tree.

And the snow came thudding down, ahead of the toppling, crashing branches, showering Kirstie and Lisa with heavy chunks, so that they had to put up their arms to protect their heads.

Then there was a blinding flash.

The falling tree hit a cable. It snapped it in two, sent the exposed ends snaking through the blue-black air, setting up an electrical charge that lit the whole sky above the girls' heads.

And the live cable snaked, coiled and flashed with many thousands of volts. It made a pattern of sparks which descended through the branches.

Lisa and Kirstie crouched below, two tiny hunched figures in a crashing landscape alive with flashing, lethal electricity.

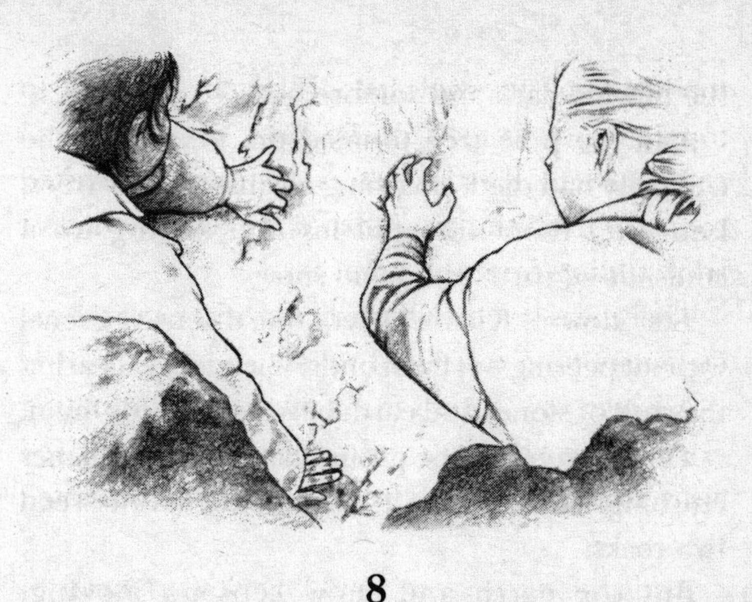

8

The tree toppled and the cable flashed.

At the last split second, as the raw ends plummeted towards the ground, carrying their killer volts, Kirstie had the presence of mind to throw herself against Lisa and bundle them both behind a ledge of rock where they sprawled full-length, hands over their heads.

The cable wrapped itself around the tall tree, then hit the ground, earthing its giant load of electricity into the snow-covered mountain. The ground absorbed the sparks with a hiss, deadening the flash of yellow light, leaving the hillside dark and sombre.

And the pine tree toppled on, long after the elecricity had died, smashing against smaller trees, knocking them like skittles and setting up a landslide of earth, mud and snow.

'Stay down!' Kirstie yelled. She'd sensed events without peering out from under their ledge, hearing the rush of stones and earth heading towards them.

The big tree hit the ground at last, its branches crashing and settling, its trunk jammed between two rocks.

But the earth and snow kept on moving, sweeping smaller pine-branches along, rolling stones down the snowy slope, gathering force until the avalanche tipped over the ledge where Lisa and Kirstie lay.

The sliding earth and snow gave way to gravity, while Kirstie's quick thinking kept them safe. As the main force of the landslide tumbled on down the slope, it left a pocket of dark space under the ledge.

The girls could make out the rush of debris scraping past their faces. Made up of logs and stones, it set up a thunderous roar in their ears.

But they stayed safely out of its path, waiting until the movement stopped until they dared to reach out and examine the layer of rubble which had jammed against the ledge.

Safe but trapped, it seemed.

'We're buried!' Lisa gasped, feeling with her fingertips the barrier which had built up between them and the outside world. Staving off a wave of panic, she grasped for any nearby object which might help them dig their way out into the fresh air, laying hold of a stout stick with which she began to chip away at the snow and earth.

Kirstie too realised that they had to dig themselves out fast, before the oxygen in their cavity was used up. She started with her bare hands, clawing away at the frozen rubble. 'It seems lighter over here!' she cried, scrabbling to clear a way towards the daylight.

And soon Lisa joined her, jabbing with her stick through twelve inches or more of packed snow.

After five frantic minutes they broke through. Lisa's stick burst through the barrier and sent clumps of snow and earth trickling back towards them.

'Careful!' Kirstie feared a cave-in which could bury them deeper than before.

So though they could see daylight and breathe fresh air, Lisa crouched back and let Kirstie scrape gently with her hands, creating a gap through the debris large enough for them to squeeze their bodies through without bringing more of the landslide toppling in on them. 'You first!' she whispered to Lisa when she thought the hole was large enough.

Holding her breath, Lisa crept out through the excavated channel, squeezing her shoulders through then hauling the rest of her body clear.

Meanwhile, Kirstie protected herself from the falling pebbles and lumps of icy snow.

There was a pause of a few seconds, then Lisa's face appeared in the opening. 'Now you!' she called, waiting for Kirstie to ease her shoulders clear of the trap, then hooking her hands under her armpits and pulling strongly. Soon they were both free.

And the scene around them was pure devastation. Trees had keeled over at odd angles, half-uprooted, threatening to fall further in the strong wind. The giant ponderosa pine had tumbled head-down, its broad trunk charred black where the massive electric current had caught it as the cables snaked and fell. And still the snow fell and the wind blew in a seemingly never-ending blizzard.

'Are you OK? Did you get hurt?' Lisa asked anxiously.

'I'm fine. How about you?' Relief at escaping from the potential death-trap made Kirstie feel energised.

'Fine. A couple of bruises . . . nothing.' Seemingly more shocked and shaky, Lisa staggered away from the ledge, straight into a dangerously unstable sapling.

The young tree collapsed under her weight, making her slide waist-deep into a drift.

Kirstie hauled her out. 'C'mon; the sooner we get to Lone Elm, the better.'

So Lisa collected herself and they staggered on, counting every step of the way, looking out for a sign that they had at last reached their destination.

'Are we there yet?' Lisa gasped, stumbling through the snow, almost at the end of her strength.

'Yeah, I see the entrance!' Kirstie cried, as the trademark tall elm tree appeared through the snowstorm. Beneath the tree was the wooden arch and the swinging sign that told visitors that they had reached the trailer park.

'Oh Jeez!' Lisa sobbed, her legs wobbling, her voice choked. 'Just show me a warm log fire and stick a mug of hot chocolate in my hands, please!'

Supporting her through the entrance and out of the snow under the porch of the reception building,

Kirstie called out to let Lennie Goodman know they were there.

There was no reply from inside the office, and when Kirstie peered through the window, she could see a tidy, empty desk but not Lennie.

'I guess he's tucked up nice and warm in his cabin.' Lisa launched herself from the porch in the direction of her grandpa's snug wooden house across a snow-covered lawn from the reception building. But her legs refused to support her and she collapsed in a heap in the snow.

'You stay here,' Kirstie ordered, heaving Lisa back on to the porch and making her sit on the step. 'I'll go find your grandpa.'

So she went across the lawn alone and knocked on Lennie's cabin door. Once again there was no sign of the old man, except, when Kirstie looked more closely, a set of footprints leaving the cabin and making their way up along the row of trailers.

Not too recent, to judge by the blurred outlines. Which meant that Lennie had left the warmth of the cabin to trudge out into the snow some time earlier, but for what reason Kirstie couldn't tell.

'What happened? Is something wrong?' Lisa called across the clearing.

'No, nothing. You stay there. Lennie's up at the trailers. I'll go find him!'

Kirstie made her way as agilely as she could through the snow, following the fading footprints past the first three trailers, then taking a right turn towards a fenced-in service area behind.

Maybe Lennie had discovered a fault in the oil-fired system which provided heat to his cabin and office. Or maybe the problem was with the electricity generator he used whenever there was a general power cut in the area.

Yes, of course. The cables were down. The power was out. Lennie would have to switch to the private source.

'Hey?' she called gently, so as not to surprise the old man. She stepped through a gap in the high fence.

And that was where she found Lisa's grandpa.

He lay slumped against the inside of the fence, against a snow-covered tarpaulin which protected the generator when it wasn't in use. The tarpaulin was half-off the machine, still grasped in Lennie's hand, partly covering his motionless form.

Kirstie fell on to her knees beside him. 'Lennie!' she cried. The first thing she did was to remove his round glasses and wipe them clear of snow. As she put them back on to his lined, unshaven face, she stroked the flakes from his forehead and cheeks.

He heard her call his name and flickered his eyelids open.

Thank heavens! Seeing that he was still alive, Kirstie hauled the tarpaulin free of the generator and used it to cover the whole of the old man's body. 'Can you move?' she asked him.

Slowly he shook his head. 'How come you showed up?'

'It's a long story. But tell me what happened. What should I do?'

'I came out to switch on the generator and found that it was broke. Then like a stupid fool, I lost my footing and slipped. Nothing to it; I fell and hit my head against the oil tank. Must've knocked myself out, darn it!'

'And you really can't move?' Relieved as she was, Kirstie still felt concerned about lifting Lennie from the ground. After all, he was heavy – maybe one hundred and eighty pounds – too much for her to lift single-handed. And she was afraid he might already be suffering from hypothermia. He oughtn't to lie in the snow any longer than she could help.

'I got this bad pain right across my back,' Lennie confessed.

'Can you move your legs?'

He tried without success, flashing Kirstie a scared look before he hid what he was feeling with another attempt at jokiness. 'Best bring my bed out here for the night, don't you think?'

Kirstie stood up. 'Wait, I'll go call the doctor!'

'You got a radio with you?' Lennie asked, his mind working well even if his body refused to comply.

'No.'

'The phones are down,' he told her. 'No power, no phone lines; not until the riggers get out here to repair the cables.'

'Right.' Of course; that was what he was doing out here in the storm in the first place. 'OK, I'll bring more blankets. And let me tell Lisa what happened. Don't worry, between us we'll figure this out!'

Lennie nodded briefly, but winced then groaned as he tried to twist and turn to see where his granddaughter could be.

'Lisa's on the porch at Reception,' she explained. 'We've been out in the blizzard for a couple of hours, getting ourselves well and truly lost. You can't imagine how glad we were to see this place!'

'But she's OK?' Letting the tarpaulin fall over him, Lennie shivered, then groaned again.

He was in a lot of pain, Kirstie realised. And he'd lost the sensation in his legs. This could turn out to be really serious. 'Wait!' she repeated. 'Give me two minutes to fetch the blankets.'

And she ran off blindly into the snow, frantically composing a few sentences to tell Lisa.

'Your grandpa had an accident,' she gasped quickly when she got to the porch. 'It's OK, he's conscious and thinking clearly. But he hurt his back and there's a danger of him freezing if we leave him where he is. So what do we do; try to carry him into his cabin?'

Lisa gasped and tried once more to get to her feet. This time, she didn't even make it for a couple of steps, but half-fainted right back into the porch.

So it was down to Kirstie. Taking off her own jacket to wrap it around Lisa's shoulders, she gave her friend a strict instruction not to move until she came back to fetch her. Double-checking that she understood, she ran off again to Lennie's cabin and dived in to gather warm blankets from his bed, then out again into the snow, wishing in vain that it would ease, and still not sure how she was going to get the old man out of the storm.

She found him, eyes closed again, and this time definitely drifting into hypothermia, despite his tarpaulin cover. As she called his name, his eyes flickered open, but there was no recognition in them, and no attempt to pretend that things would work out.

'Lennie, wake up!' she pleaded as his eyes slowly shut without him having spoken. She took away the stiff and dirty canvas cover, replacing it with blankets and a down-filled counterpane. Then she put the tarpaulin back on top to keep out the snow. 'It's important; don't fall asleep!'

Once more the old man forced his eyes open. 'I hear you!' he whispered.

'Stay awake! I can't help you if you lose consciousness. I need to know what to do!'

He nodded and sighed. 'Where's Lisa?'

'She's OK. Listen, Lennie, I can't lift you. If I keep the blankets wrapped around you, can you at least try to stand?'

Slowly he shook his head. His eyelids drooped.

And Kirstie realised that it was hopeless to try to get the old man to move under his own steam. She needed extra help. Maybe if she was straight with Lisa about how sick Lennie was, then Lisa would make a huge effort to overcome her own weakness just for the time it took to help Lennie indoors.

'Stay awake!' This time she needed to be rough

to rouse him from his semi-conscious state. Shaking him by the shoulders, she patted hard at his cheeks until he opened his eyes. 'Tell yourself a story. Start counting to a hundred. Just don't drift off, OK!'

'One – two – three . . .' His slurred voice tried to count.

'. . . Four – five – six . . .' She still heard him as she stood up and backed out of the service yard.

Then she turned into the snowstorm to come face to face with the two figures she least expected to see.

'Starlight!' she gasped.

The horse stood quietly in the whirling flakes. His pale mane was clogged with ice, his legs and belly covered with packed snow. And he looked at her with his dark, deep eyes, head up, enduring whatever Jay asked him to endure.

And there was Jay too, equally silent at first. He stood beside his horse, loosely holding the reins, his face half obscured by the upturned collar of his thin denim jacket. He stared at Kirstie, obviously aware of the emergency she faced over Lennie.

'I need your help!' she gasped, stepping aside to give Jay a clear view of the prostrate form.

'I know it.' A rapid nod, a brisk move to clear the worst of the snow from Starlight's saddle. 'Do we risk moving him? Or should I ride out of here to fetch a doctor?'

'He won't last out here in the cold much longer. I guess we have to try lifting him.' Storing all her questions for later, Kirstie sprang into action, turning round to go back and raise the old man's head from the ground. 'I'm hoping that it's the cold that's got to him and numbed his feet and legs, not that he actually broke his back or anything.'

'You'd better believe it,' Jay agreed. He too must have thought it was worth the risk. Edging Starlight closer towards the gap in the fence, he turned the patient horse sideways on and waited for Kirstie to make her next move.

'Lennie's too weak to sit in the saddle, so we have to try and sling him across, face down,' she decided. 'Will Starlight be able to stand still while we do that?'

'Easy, boy,' Jay murmured into the horse's ear, calmly stroking his cheek, then coming to join Kirstie. 'We both crouch down, one to either side. We sling the old guy's arms along our shoulders, like so. OK?'

Crouching ready to take her half of Lennie's weight, Kirstie nodded.

'So we lift,' Jay ordered quietly.

As the old man moaned and sighed with pain, they raised him up until they stood upright.

'He's heavy!' Kirstie gasped. Her shoulder strained fit to snap in two.

'Quick, ease him across to Starlight,' Jay said.

Between them they did it.

'You gotta hold him while I duck down and hoist him up into the saddle,' Jay told her, quickly doing it before she had time to think.

One second, two seconds, holding the full weight of a semi-conscious man . . .

Jay crouched and lifted. Lennie slid easily over

Starlight's back. The horse took on the weight and stood steady.

'Walk on!' Jay ordered with a soft click of his tongue.

Starlight stepped out through the snow, sure-footed and determined. He bore his burden with ease, carrying the old man out of the cold into the life-restoring warmth of his log cabin.

9

'How come?' was Kirstie's big question after she and Jay had managed to ease Lennie on to his big leather sofa in front of a low fire.

'How come me and Starlight showed up when we were needed?' He shook his head and gave a short grunt. 'I'll explain later. You make the old guy comfortable while I go fetch Lisa.'

And Jay shot out of the cabin while Kirstie piled new logs into the grate, satisfied to hear the crack of sparks in the embers and to see small flames flare up and catch hold. Blue smoke rose up the chimnney and the smell of pine resin filled the room.

Soon Jay returned with a shivering, shaky Lisa. He helped her inside and sat her down by the fire, then he quickly vanished outside once more.

Kirstie hurried to her friend's side. 'How are you doing?' she asked anxiously.

'Just great!' Lisa huddled inside the extra jacket Kirstie had given her, her teeth chattering, her hands shaking as they grasped the edges of the jacket across her chest. She gave a small gasp when she spotted Lennie lying flat out on the sofa, almost hidden by a pile of blankets.

'Don't panic!' the old man said faintly. 'I just seem to have a little problem getting my legs to work is all.'

'Grandpa!' Weakly Lisa stood up and went to his side. 'How can I help? What do you need?'

'A shot of whiskey would be good!' he grinned, putting on a brave front. 'But they don't recommend that for hypothermia, more's the pity.'

Realising that the fire was helping to restore Lennie to full consciousness, Kirstie's mind flew on. 'Where did Jay just go?' she muttered to herself, dashing out on to the narrow porch to see.

Outside, she saw that the gale force winds were easing at last and that the snow was falling more gently. It was even possible that the sky was lighter and the clouds lifting. But maybe that was just wishful thinking. In any case, she had to corner Jay before he took it into his head to vanish with Starlight once more.

Luckily, she didn't have far to look. The kid and his horse were around the side of Lennie's cabin, close to a low shelter where the old man stacked his store of winter logs.

'Help me empty this,' Jay grunted as soon as he realised she was there. 'C'mon, don't just stand there. We need the logs out and Starlight in before night falls!'

So she set to, liting the heavy logs from the neat stack and casting them to one side of the shelter, while the unsaddled sorrel horse stood patiently under a nearby tree. He watched with sagging head, his thin sides still heaving from his recent struggle through the blizzard.

'We need to get him under this shelter pretty darned fast,' Jay urged, hauling logs off the stack. 'Does Lisa's grandpa have any straw and hay we could use?'

'I doubt it.' Kirstie knew that Lennie didn't keep a horse at the trailer park and so would have no use for the bedding or the feed.

'Bad news,' Jay muttered, straining to carry as

many logs as he could take all in one go. He threw the pile down to the ground with a clatter. 'Starlight's pretty well done in. He needs food fast.'

Kirstie nodded and sighed, as if this was the final straw. 'So go ahead, hit me with another problem.'

'OK. We're completely cut off,' he reminded her. 'We've no power since the cables came down . . .'

'How did you know that?' she broke in.

'I was there. I saw it.'

'So, how come?' This time she had him cornered to give his explanation, talking as he worked to empty the shelter.

'So it's a stupid story,' he admitted. 'I'm in the hospital and I get this idea into my head that Starlight is out here in the mountains, pining for me.'

'That's not stupid,' Kirstie interrupted again. 'That's the way it was. Only, I'd been getting him to take food over the last twenty-four hours. He was coming to trust me a little bit.'

'Hmm.' Jay stopped work to stare intently at her.

She looked back as long as she could hold the gaze, then turned away to heave another log from the stack. 'So carry on!'

'So I cut loose from the hospital, borrow my dad's pick-up and drive straight out here in the middle of the night. OK, so it's crazy; I just want one look at my horse. Maybe the last ever.'

'Don't say that,' Kirstie told him quietly.

'Whatever. I didn't figure on Starlight's reaction to my visit. Once he sees me, he sets up this snickering and neighing which is disturbing all the other horses in the barn. And it gets worse when it looks like I'm getting ready to go.'

'Right.' She could easily picture the sorrel's reluctance to let Jay leave. 'So your solution is to take him with you?'

'Yeah. Smart, huh? I fetch him a saddle from the tack-room and we set out into the snow, who knows where!'

'OK, I got all that.' By this time, the shelter was almost empty and they'd created enough space for Jay to lead Starlight inside. 'We know you headed along the side of the creek because me and Lisa picked up your trail. But when did you figure out we were following you?'

'Pretty soon after you crossed the creek,' he admitted. 'And by this time, I didn't have a clue where I was. So I figured the smart thing to do was to hide and wait for you and Lisa to give up the search and go back home. Then I could take my own time to say my goodbyes to Starlight then ride back to the ranch, following in your footsteps.'

Leading the horse gently from the tree into the shelter, Jay let Starlight take his time to sniff around and settle in his mind that the dark space was safe.

'Not so smart, as it turned out,' Kirstie told him. 'Because once the blizzard set in, Lisa and I got ourselves totally lost down those draws and gulleys. It was like the blind leading the blind!'

'I just guessed you two must know your way around!' He smiled wryly. 'Instead of which, you cause me and my horse to almost fry in a million volts of live electricity!'

'How close were you?'

'Too close. I saw the whole firework show from about a hundred yards back. Starlight spooked so bad, he reared up and threw me off. The first time in my life that ever happened.'

Meanwhile, she and Lisa had been digging themselves out of a mini landslide. As Jay looked around for something to draw across the low entrance to the shelter to form a windbreak, Kirstie ran to fetch the discarded tarpaulin which she'd used earlier to protect Lennie from the worst of the cold. She hooked it along a row of giant nails sticking out from a supporting beam and pretty soon had constructed an effective screen.

'So, you didn't get hurt when Starlight threw you?' By this time she had almost the complete picture.

'Nope. I landed in some soft snow, and the little guy stuck around while I got back on my feet. I figure he was kinda sorry about it. Anyhow, by the time you two girls were back on track, we were following you again. Which is how come I was there to help with Lisa's grandpa.'

And now that Starlight was safely out of the snow, they knew that they needed to head back inside to see how Lisa and Lennie were doing.

So they left the brave little sorrel, still shaking and shivering after his ordeal, and went indoors to find Lisa boiling a kettle of water on the log fire and searching the place from top to bottom to gather all the candles and oil lamps she could find.

'We're gonna need these when night draws in,' she explained, lining them up along the window-sill. 'And I've checked the food situation. We've got a little bread, cookies, cheese, plenty of raw vegetables . . .'

'Hold it!' Kirstie interrupted. 'Do we have carrots?'

'Yeah, and celery. And I guess we might have broccoli too.'

'Look in the rack by the back door,' Lennie

advised from his position on the sofa. The old man hadn't moved since they'd brought him inside. He lay stiff, afraid to move because of the pain in his back.

So Kirstie went into the kitchen and returned with an armful of vegetables. 'Horses can eat all of this stuff,' she said as she handed them over to Jay. 'I guess Starlight gets a surprise gourmet supper!'

Gladly he took the food out to the shelter, leaving the girls and Lennie to make more preparations for an overnight stay.

'It's like we're under siege,' Lennie grumbled from under his pile of blankets. His glasses glinted in the firelight as he watched Kirstie pile more logs into the grate. 'Candles and cookies. No power. But we're all pulling together pretty well, so I guess we'll make it.'

'But I'm worried about you,' Lisa confessed. Time to rest and recover her strength meant she was back on her feet, while the old man still lay without moving a muscle.

'Well don't be. I can wiggle my toes now; look!'

Lifting the blankets off his feet, Lisa saw that the messages were getting through from his brain. 'Can you feel me touching your ankle?'

Lennie nodded. 'See; things are looking good!'

'For everyone except Jay,' Kirstie added quietly, looking first at the closed door to make sure that he couldn't overhear. 'The longer this goes on without us being able to contact anyone, the worse his chances are.'

Demanding an explanation, Lennie listened closely to the details about Jay's illness and the imminent bone marrow transplant.

'You say he's lined up to have this thing done tomorrow?' the old man repeated in a shocked whisper.

Kirstie nodded. 'But he doesn't know that. He was told he would have to wait until after Christmas. That's why he cut loose from the hospital.'

'And you see how much he cares for Starlight!' Lisa added. 'As a matter of fact, I figure he'd die for that horse!'

'Don't!' Kirstie shuddered. The idea was too close to reality. 'How are we gonna find a way to get him out of here and back to the hospital in Denver?'

Her question met a long silence, while the logs in the grate blazed and the flames flickered uneven light across the darkening room.

'How long until nightfall?' Lisa asked.

'Two, maybe three hours,' Lennie replied. 'After that there's not a hope of getting Jay out.'

'How would we do it anyways?' Kirstie wondered. 'No way can Starlight battle back out of here. The poor guy's totally exhausted as it is.'

'Could you and Jay make it on foot?' Lisa shot the idea at Kirstie, then regretted it. 'No, forget I said that. It's way too difficult to find your route, as I know only too well!'

'I guess we could try,' Kirstie said slowly. Though if she was honest, she would have to admit that her own legs and arms felt too heavy and tired to trek any distance through the snow.

'No!' Lennie said. 'I won't be responsible for telling Sandy you didn't make it through, OK!'

So that idea was out, and they could hear Jay returning from the shelter, his footsteps echoing on the hollow boards of the front porch.

He opened the door and beckoned Kirstie and Lisa to come outside. 'Take a look at this!' he said eagerly.

Out on the porch they saw the usual silent, white wilderness. A few slow flakes drifted down from the lifting clouds. Otherwise the scene was still.

'Don't you hear that?' Jay whispered, his excitement rising. 'Starlight does. Just come and see!'

So they waded through the snow to the makeshift

stable and found the horse with his ears pricked, looking out from the shelter and gazing up into the clouds.

'What can he hear?' Lisa said, still puzzled.

'Listen!' Jay insisted.

Kirstie concentrated. She heard the last of the wind sighing through the tall trees behind the trailer park, but nothing else. Unless . . . unless!

Quickly she ran on to the snow-covered clearing in front of Lennie's cabin. She gazed up at the grey sky, hoping against hope.

She heard a a low, distant whir of something mechanical. An engine in the sky. A chugging, churning sound growing nearer.

'Helicopter!' Jay whispered.

She nodded. No doubt about it. Maybe an emergency chopper carrying riggers to fix the broken power lines over Bear Hunt Overlook? Maybe even Ricky Thornton and his rescue team out from San Luis now that the weather had eased?

Kirstie glanced at Lisa to see that she too had identified the sound.

'Cool!' A smile hovered around Lisa's lips.

'I knew it!' Jay whispered.

And the helicopter appeared over a far ridge, emerging from the clouds like a clumsy insect, its metal body tilting and turning as it hovered over a carpet of snow-laden trees.

'Come this way!' Lisa prayed out loud, begging their first link with the outside world to approach. 'Hey, they're turning away!' she cried in alarm, as the helicopter pilot seemed to manoeuvre his craft and swing out along the ridge in the opposite direction.

Their hopes sank.

'This way!' Lisa yelled a second time.

But the passengers in the chopper looked down on a vast white wilderness. Lisa, Kirstie and Jay couldn't make any signal big enough to attract their attention.

'Come back!' Kirstie whispered, her heart in her mouth as the tiny helicopter chugged away slowly along the distant ridge. 'Come back, please!'

10

'Steady down!' Lennie advised the three kids from his position on the sofa.

They'd dashed inside with devastated faces to explain what had happened.

'They couldn't see us from that distance!' Lisa cried, her hopes of rescue for Jay shattered. 'We were way too small for the guys in the chopper to pick out from up there!'

'Easy,' Lennie repeated. 'What you say is true. But we're not through yet.'

Kirstie seized on the glimmer of hope. 'What d'you mean?'

'I mean, we have to hope that this is the rescue team from San Luis and not the cable riggers,' Lennie said slowly and calmly. 'All the electricity company guys are looking out for is a broken line. Once they find it, they'll land, do the job, then pack up and go home.'

'But if it's Ricky Thornton?'

'If it's the rescue team and they've been sent out to find Jay, like you said, then they keep looking until they find him.'

'So they'll fly back over.' Kirstie grabbed at the possibility. 'And next time we have to be good and ready.'

Lennie nodded. 'How are we gonna make contact; any ideas?'

Standing thoughtfully in a group around his sofa, Kirstie threw out the idea of using a light as a signal to attract the chopper's attention. 'For starters, Lennie's generator's been knocked out, as we know. So no chance of rigging up any kind of electrical beam and directing it towards the sky.

'Second, a bonfire won't cut it either. One, it takes too long to build and set alight. Two, every scrap of wood is buried beneath four feet of snow!'

'Except the stack of logs we threw out of the shelter,' Jay reminded her, ready to run with the idea of lighting a fire as a signal.

But Lisa jumped in with a better idea. 'Grandpa, where do you store the giant flags you raise over the entrance during the summer season?'

'In my bedroom, in a trunk under the bed.' Trying to prop himself on his elbows, he watched as she dashed to find them.

Lisa soon returned with a neat pile of brightly-coloured, silky fabric.

'What are they for?' Kirstie asked, stepping back as Lisa took the top flag from the pile and shook it out to its full extent.

The Stars and Stripes was practically as big as the ten-foot-square room.

'Whoa!' Lennie complained from beneath the silk banner. He edged it from his face with a quizzical look.

'Sorry, Grandpa!' Gathering it back in, Lisa turned to Jay and Kirstie. 'There are four of these flags, all different. There's the Stars and Stripes, the Colorado state flag . . .'

'Yeah, yeah, but what do we do with them?' Kirstie wanted to know.

Lisa thrust the first flag into her arms. 'Bring it outside. And Jay, you take this one. Follow me!'

They did as they were told, running out after her

on to the wide stretch of open space between the cabin and the trailer-park entrance.

'Spread them out flat as you can!' Lisa ordered. Lay all four to make a giant square that the chopper can spot from way up!'

'Got it!' Jay set to eagerly. When he found that the corners of the Colorado flag lifted and curled in the wind, he ran to fetch logs from the discarded heap next to Starlight's shelter.

Soon all four flags were stretched out and anchored at the corners to make a twenty-foot square patchwork of bright colour on the pure white clearing.

Lisa stood back. 'What d'you think; will it work?'

'I figure we have a chance to find out right now,' Kirstie replied, noticing Starlight emerge from his shelter, ears pricked, gazing up at the sky. 'It seems like the pilot is taking a second look at Bear Hunt Overlook.'

And sure enough, they soon heard the faint whir of helicopter blades, then saw the awkward-looking craft tilt and rise over the horizon.

'This time we *are* ready!' Lisa said firmly. 'If they don't see a weird patch of red and blue amongst all this white stuff, all I can say is those guys need an eye-test!'

*   *   *

'Good job!' Ricky Thornton told them. He especially congratulated Lisa for thinking so fast. Above the roar of the helicopter blades which had whipped the silk flags from their anchorage and blown them across the clearing, right up against the cabin porch, the rescue team leader took in both the problem and what needed to be done.

'Mike and Terry, you take care of Lennie, OK? Put him in a body brace and lift him out of there fast as you can.'

Two men in white helmets and green paramedic suits jumped from the chopper carrying a full medical kit. They disappeared inside the cabin to tend to the patient.

'We thought you weren't gonna see us a second time!' Lisa confessed. 'You almost turned round before you reached us. I tell you, I yelled and shouted until my throat hurt!'

Ricky, a tall, well-built guy of around thirty, grinned quickly. 'Didn't hear a thing,' he admitted. 'But Terry spotted the flags and made me turn back. I think his exact words were, "Didn't anybody tell those guys down there that the Fourth of July came and went six months back?"!'

His comment produced a general grin, which

soon changed to looks of concern as the paramedics emerged from the cabin with Lennie strapped inside a body-brace, being carried on a stretcher.

'Not as bad as it looks,' Lennie assured them, turning his head as the two guys hurried past. 'They think I slipped a disc is all.'

'Could a slipped disc be that painful?' Kirstie asked Ricky.

He nodded. 'Lack of mobility in the lower body was probably down to hypothermia. But don't worry, we'll take all the films and put him through the scans as soon as we get him to hospital. With a bit of luck, and some intensive physiotherapy, we should have him back on his feet pretty soon.'

'My mom will go crazy with him,' Lisa told them. 'She's always telling him that no way should he spend his winters out here all alone. Now she has the ammunition to prove it.'

'Not that he'll listen to common sense, most probably.' Ricky knew these stubborn old-timers and how they stuck with their backwoods routines. Turning to Jay, he asked him if there was anything he needed to fetch from the cabin before he too climbed into the helicopter.

Jay turned his head to one side and shrugged. 'I'm not planning to go anywhere,' he said quietly.

The rescue team leader frowned. 'Run that by me one more time, would you?'

'I said I'm not leaving,' Jay repeated.

Lisa's eyebrows shot up in surprise and she grabbed Kirstie by the arm. 'Uh-oh!' she whispered.

'So I come all the way out here, risk my crew's lives on the tail-end of a blizzard, only to hear that you don't feel like being rescued after all?' Ricky Thornton was quickly and obviously running out of patience.

'He's fretting over his horse,' Kirstie explained. 'That's what started this whole thing. I can understand that he doesn't want to abandon Starlight.'

'Who's abandoning who? What are we talking about; some dumb horse, right?' Ricky glanced at his wristwatch to check how much daylight they had left. 'Listen, I don't intend to hang around until dark, then run my chopper into the nearest mountain. Either Jay gets in right now, or we leave without him!'

Jay narrowed his eyes, ready to walk away, but Kirstie broke free from Lisa to take hold of his shoulder. 'Jay, you need to go with them,' she said quietly and urgently. 'Your blood results were good yesterday. They say you can go ahead and have the transplant tomorrow!'

A small shudder ran through him. 'Tomorrow?'

She nodded. 'Earlier than they thought. Jay, this is your big chance to get better. Don't throw it away!'

'But what about Starlight?' He pulled free of her, heading towards the makeshift stable, where the sorrel horse stood watching quietly. He'd almost made it across the clearing when Kirstie intercepted him a second time.

'Let *me* take care of Starlight,' she said firmly.

Jay shook his head. 'If I leave, he'll think I'm dumping him for good.'

'He won't. I'll talk to him. I'll let him know you'll be back.'

Again he shook his head. 'He needs me.'

'Sure. He needs you to get well and come back to fetch him.' Kirstie took what he said and twisted it. She didn't let up. 'What's gonna happen to Starlight if you don't get your treatment? You're gonna die and he's gonna pine big-time!'

Jay let out a rapid sigh. He closed his eyes for a second and hung his head.

'Really, Jay, I can take care of things until you come out of the hospital. The horse trusts me.'

Sure, Starlight trusted her, but would he know what was happening if Jay tried to climb into the chopper? It was a lot to expect. But Kirstie had to convince Jay that it was true.

'I'll get proper feed to him. I'll keep him warm. I'll do everything you would do,' she insisted. 'And I'll call you in Denver just as soon as I get him out of here.'

Jay looked up at her. 'That's a promise?'

She met his gaze and nodded back. 'Promise.'

So he took a last lingering look at Starlight, then turned swiftly on his heel. He ran to the helicopter and let Mike and Terry haul him up into its belly.

Ricky climbed into the cockpit. The hatches slid shut.

'Easy, Starlight!' Kirstie took the horse's halter rope and held him steady.

The little sorrel rolled his eyes and laid his ears flat. He pulled his head away with all his might, raising his front feet off the ground as the chopper blades whirred fast and the machine started to shift then lift off the ground.

'Wait!' Lisa ran across the clearing after it, her clothes tugged by the high wind raised by the blades. She waved both arms in a frantic signal for Ricky to lean out of the cockpit.

Meanwhile, Kirstie struggled to keep a hold of Starlight's rope. For a second, she thought she

would lose the battle, that he would pull free and race after Jay, and that Jay wouldn't be able to bear the sight of the frantic horse.

He would jump back out of the chopper and all her persuasion would come to nothing. 'Jeez, Lisa!' she complained to herself. 'Just let them leave, for Chrissake!'

'We need a radio!' Lisa yelled above the roar of the helicopter's engine. In the rush to make an exit, nobody had thought of leaving the essential piece of equipment. 'Throw one down!'

Ricky strained to hear, then nodded. A moment later, after he'd reached inside the cockpit, he held out a small, square black object which he then aimed and threw.

Lisa dived forward to catch it.

And Kirstie held on to Starlight, tugging him back down to the ground, shortening his lead-rope until she could hook her fingers through the halter itself and hold him steady.

'It's OK,' she breathed, watching the 'copter take off at last. 'Jay wants me to take care of you. We'll radio through to the Forest Rangers to bring hay for you to eat. As soon as the ploughs can clear a way to drive a trailer through, we'll have you out of here!'

* * *

'Ready?' Sandy Scott asked. She'd poked her head inside the barn to find Kirstie still busy with brush and comb. 'Hey, if you groom that little horse any more, you'll rub all the hair off his back!'

'I want him to look special,' she insisted. 'Anyway, did they get here yet?'

'Bonnie just pulled up in Lennie's trailer.'

'Then I'll be out in couple of minutes,' Kirstie promised.

She'd been up early to get Starlight in prime condition; as good as he could be in his thick winter coat at the end of a long, cold January. The dawn was pink over the white peaks of the mountains, then the sky had turned a clear eggshell blue.

It was the day they'd all been waiting for and that had been so long coming.

Giving Starlight one last brush from head to toe, Kirstie reviewed the past month.

Ricky Thornton had got Lennie and Jay into hospital before nightfall on the day before Christmas Eve. His prediction about the old man's injury had proved correct – a simple slipped disc and no permanent damage due to hypothermia. Lennie had been forced to have complete bed-rest and to agree to spend the rest of the winter in town with Bonnie.

And Jay had received his vital treatment. It was long and painful, and had left him very weak. Afterwards, they'd kept him in isolation for weeks to avoid infection. He'd seen the world through sterile glass walls. Chuck and Marie had visited in white hospital gowns and masks.

Meanwhile, back at the trailer park . . .

Lisa had used the radio to contact Smiley Gilpin and his team of rangers.

'We need food!' she'd told them. '. . . No, not food for ourselves; I mean, horse-food! Oh, and bring a couple of bales of straw while I think about it.'

The Forest Ranger had responded promptly to the unusual request. He'd stopped off at Red Eagle Lodge to pick up a bale of the best alfalfa and two of straw, then with his snow-truck and plough he'd forged a way through the drifts to the trailer park.

Dusk had been drawing in as the giant truck appeared at the snow-clogged entrance. Smiley and one other ranger had jumped out and unloaded Starlight's supplies.

Kirstie and Lisa had rushed with it straight into the horse's shelter.

'Now eat!' Kirstie had ordered, stretching out and

offering him a handful of the sweetest, cleanest hay. 'Jay's gone to hospital for treatment, and we need you to be good and strong when he comes out!'

The little Polish Arab had looked keenly at her with his coal-dark eyes. The white star on his forehead had shone in the darkness. He'd thought about it, tilting his beautiful head this way and that. Then he'd reached out and started to munch.

'So this is your big day!' she told Starlight now, putting down the brush at last.

She could hear voices in the yard: Matt asking Chuck North about his new job with Donna Rose, Chuck replying that it was good and that his new boss knew a thing or two about beef farming. On top of which, she'd permitted the Norths to bring Starlight over to the Circle R just as soon as Jay was well enough to look after him.

'I'm gonna lead you out now, OK?' Kirstie said nervously to the suddenly fidgety horse. 'Yeah, you're right; that's Chuck's voice you can hear. Bonnie and Lisa are out there with him, along with Marie.'

Starlight swished his tail against the side of the stall and shuffled impatiently towards the exit.

Kirstie held him back for one last second to

straighten out his silky mane. 'Oh, and did I mention Jay? He's there too, as if you didn't know!'

So proudly she walked the eager horse out along the dark central aisle of the barn, through the wide wooden doors into the cold, blue day.

Starlight pranced and danced in the light. His coat shone copper-coloured, his mane hung smoothly against his arched neck.

'That's one good-looking horse!' Chuck North admitted, as the whole crowd of onlookers murmured their admiration.

And Jay stepped forward from the rest, tall and pale after his weeks in isolation, with eyes only for Starlight, his dancing, daintily-stepping Arab.

Kirstie had to hold back the tears as she handed over the lead-rope.

'You kept your promise,' Jay whispered. 'The little guy never looked better!'

She thought of the weeks of feeding, brushing, combing, picking out hooves, and exercising in the trodden snow of the arena. She'd grown to love the little horse as her own. And he in turn had given her his total trust.

'You're welcome,' she said now as she let go of the lead-rope.

A couple of heart strings broke right there and

then. But she was proud of what she'd done. And overjoyed for Jay North.

'Hey,' he whispered in the horse's soft ear. 'Am I *glad* to see you!'

Another Hodder Children's book

HORSES OF HALF-MOON RANCH
Silver Spur

Jenny Oldfield

The ranch's new wrangler, Troy Hendren, is full of stories of his years spent cowboying in Montana and his faithful horse, Silver Spur. According to Troy, Silver Spur can spin on a ten-cent piece and understands every word he says. But oldtimer Hadley Crane is suspicious of this flashy cowboy. When a guest mislays an antique gold locket, is Hadley right in pointing the finger at Troy?